A DRUMBEAT TOO NEAR

WWII 1942

When German U-Boats Lurked off Cape Cod

by BILL FLYNN

To Kevin
Best Wishes
Bill Flynn

ISBN: I452841012
ISBN-I3: 978I452841014

ALSO BY BILL FLYNN

A Deadly Class Reunion

The Feathery

For

Kathy

Beth

Patty

Susan

Janey

and

Barbara,
their mother, my wife and best friend

ACKNOWLEDGMENTS

My sincere thanks go to the staff at the Provincetown, Massachusetts, Library and at the Highland Light Museum on Cape Cod for their assistance during my research there.

The following novels helped anchor my knowledge relating to German U-boat operations during WWII, Operation Drumbeat, and Admiral Karl Dönitz:

THE ADMIRAL'S WOLFPACK by Jean Noli

TORPEDO JUNCTION by Homer H. Hickam

OPERATION DRUMBEAT by Michael Gannon

A special thank you to artist and golfer
Angelo Marino for the sketch titled THE DUNE

"The only thing that really frightened me during the war was the submarine threat."

—Winston Churchill

AUTHOR'S NOTE

This is a novel of historical fiction. For the most part, characters and events are fictional, but in some cases, events and characterizations follow actual historical occurrences. These events are placed in the same timeframe as the fictitious happenings by the author. The historical facts coincidental with the fictional storyline may be found in Appendix A

A few Cape Cod and Southern food recipes coincidental with the storyline may be found in Appendix B.

The author dedicates this book to the memory of so many brave men lost at sea on both sides during that WWII ocean war.

CHAPTER I

Aboard German Sub U-432
North Atlantic
December 20, 1941

U-432 is cruising on the surface at fifteen knots in a calm sea one hundred and sixty-nine nautical miles East of Halifax, Nova Scotia. The submarine is part of a pack of U-boats marauding convoys staged in Halifax and destined for England or Russia. This patrol has been a long one. Fresh water and provisions are running low. Forty-three days at sea…so far, four Allied ships sunk and one damaged.

The U-432 commander, Oberleutnant Karl Heineke, is on the deck with his second in command and the chief boatswain mate. Each man holds binoculars and is scanning the horizon in all directions. As is a U-boat commander's customary dress, Karl Heineke wears a black leather coat that reaches his ankles. His cap is white, without starch, and the black bill is set low over his forehead with only enough space for the binocular eyepieces to enter.

Heineke lets the binoculars drop to his chest to be held there by a leather strap. "How're the men below doing, Number One?"

"All present and accounted for, sir." He smiles and says, "Hungry, horny, and hopefully headed homeward."

"Long cruise, Number One. Hope I can keep all of them safe until the end of this one and during the rest of this war."

"Long one, but successful, sir. Four ships sunk, twelve torpedoes launched. Be nice to make it five with the two left in the bow before docking at Lorient."

The chief boatswain's mate asks for permission to go below and the permission is granted.

Without any of the crew around to notice, the formality between the U-boat commander and his first mate is dropped. This is their fifth patrol together and many near-death experiences have made for a tight bond of friendship.

Hans Topp is a jolly, beer-drinking Bavarian when on land, but a dedicated submariner at sea. Hans's wife and three children live in Augsburg, Germany. He looks to the East. "I've missed being with the kids and wife three Christmases in a row. When will I get that chance?"

Hans's frustrated inquiry brings a more pointed question to Karl's mind about why he's in the mid-Atlantic commanding a U-boat. *I'm not enamored by the Nazi regime, only driven by the dedication of making this boat perform and caring for my crew. How did I get here? I enrolled at the Sorbonne, Paris in 1931, majoring in the French and English languages, graduating in 1934. After, I got a job as an assistant purser on a passenger liner out of Hamburg. It lasted for only one year. In 1935 my father, a World War 1 submarine officer, convinced me that another war was on the horizon and I best join the Navy instead of being drafted into the infantry. I relented and was accepted as an officer cadet. After four years of training to be a U-boat commander I was assigned to U-123 as executive officer. After five patrols with U-123 I was given command of U-432 in March of 1941.*

Karl Heineke looks from stern to bow and feels the pride in his boat and the crew that mans it. The U-432 is a Type VII/41. It's two hundred and twenty feet long and every space is taken up with equipment, provisions, and sleeping bunks. The crew sleeps and eats in shifts, and one head represents the toilet needs for the entire complement of forty-three men. The top speed surfaced is eighteen knots and eight knots when submerged. Its maximum range is six thousand five hundred nautical miles under diesel engine power and eighty nautical miles submerged under electrical power before the batteries require charging on the ocean's surface.

Two anti-aircraft guns are mounted on deck. The U-boat left port with fourteen torpedoes. There were four in the bow and in place for firing with eight stored below decks, ready to be loaded into the four tubes. One torpedo was loaded in the aft tube with another stored below it. Now, the two remaining ones in the bow are ready to be launched.

Hans breaks into Karl's thoughts with a rhetorical question, "How many more Christmases at sea, Karl?"

"Who knows how long this war will drag on? Now that the Americans are in it, it could be a shorter time." Karl then smiles and looks away from the ocean's horizon directly at his friend.

"I won't tell our Führer you said that, Karl." Hans's laugh is a deep-down belly one.

The chief boatswain mate interrupts. He pops his head up through the hatch. "An *Enigma* message just reported that U-*240* has found a convoy. They're coming our way, sir."

Hans's command is an automatic one. "Clear the deck!"

They scramble through the hatch and down the ladder. The hatch closes and a wheel turns to secure it. The captain hurries to his nook near the control room. The places that he must dodge his six-foot body and duck his head are memorized. Those reflex actions are trained by making many passages through that low overhead with its warren of pipes, gauges, and valves...all positioned to make head contact.

When he reaches the captain's nook, Karl removes his cap and runs a hand through his tightly cropped blond hair. He replaces his white cap with the visor in back so it won't interfere during his periscope viewing. He then takes a moment to look at a framed photograph on the small table beside his bunk. It's a full-featured pose by an attractive woman with the Eiffel Tower in the background.

Out loud, to the photograph, he says, "Here we go again, Marie Paul." He then leaves the captain's nook and dashes to the control room.

After being briefed on the position of the convoy, the captain studies the chart table for a minute before ordering a course correction. Hans repeats the order to the helmsman and stands by for more of them that will come at a fast pace.

"Flood ballast tanks!"

"Stern up seven degrees!"

"Bow down seven degrees!"

"Level off at periscope depth!"

"Up periscope!"

Karl Heineke bends his head to peer into the periscope eyepiece. He scans the horizon for one hundred and eighty degrees in front of the U-boat. No convoy in sight. He touches a switch that brings the periscope down below the surface and asks his radioman, "Fritz, any contact?"

Fritz is concentrating on a weak pinging sound coming through his earphones. He spins a wheel to move the antenna and finds a stronger signal. It peaks at one hundred and thirty-two degrees and he tells his captain that.

"Course correction to one hundred thirty-two degrees," is the command, followed by, "Up periscope."

A narrower section around the new heading is searched. First Karl sees smoke. His guess is that it's from a tanker that's burning after being torpedoed. Soon an outline appears through the periscope optics of at least a dozen ships in convoy formation heading toward them. The periscope comes down and a command to battle stations follows. The battle station command was not necessary, for the crew is already in that position anticipating the action. The orders to maneuver the U-boat into the torpedo-launch position come fast. The distance to the convoy is called out every ten seconds.

"Flood forward torpedo tubes one and four." Is Heineke's next command.

The periscope goes up again and Captain Heineke selects his target. It's a large tanker and the U-432's bow is positioned for a broadside hit.

"Fire one..." It's the command the crew is waiting for.

The torpedo is launched from forward tube number one and its trail of white phosphorous foam tells the captain that it's headed for the tanker at mid-ships. An explosion and large fireball confirm a direct hit. When that soundwave reaches the U-boat as an underwater muffled metallic clang, a cheer by the crew follows.

"Hans, we have that one torpedo left, but the destroyer will be searching for us. It might be best to get out of the area before he finds us... on the other hand, there's a chance for more tonnage with that last torpedo. Number One, what do you suggest?"

Hans's answer is quick. "Let's find a target for the last *eel* and hurry back to Lorient. I may get to see my kids and wife before the New Year."

Karl searches and finds a good-size cargo ship that'd scurried away from the convoy after the tanker was hit. The same firing routine brings the same result, and the same jubilation rings throughout the U-432. The cheer from the crew is for the tally of two more sunken ships for a total of six...also coupled with knowing they'd be headed back to port after this long patrol.

The excitement and noise stops when the radioman raises a hand for silence. Through his earphones he hears the pings made by a destroyer's propellers. It's heading straight for them at a range of six hundred meters. After he alerts the captain, his command rings out through the U-boat loud and clear.

"Alarm!"

It's the command to crash-dive down deeper. Ballast tanks are completely blown and hydroplanes fore and aft are positioned for a steep dive. All crewmembers not on a control station rush forward toward the bow so their weight will enhance the dive angle.

"Level off at one hundred fifty meters," is the captains next command. "We'll see what this fellow *has*. All engines stop...make this a quiet boat, men."

The sonar operator has the direction-finder antenna positioned on the approaching destroyer and says, "Captain, he's closing fast. Range is three hundred meters."

"Rig for depth charges."

That order from the captain makes the crew scurry through the boat to perform their much-practiced task of securing equipment and turning some valves to a closed position.

The captain soon finds out what the destroyer *has* when the first salvo of depth charges float down to detonate on the port and starboard side of U-432. There isn't a direct hit during the first volley, but the concussions jar the boat with menacing jolts. After about a dozen near-misses, there's a pause.

"Okay, he's made his first pass...he'll be back," says Heineke, following that with a request for a damage report.

The engineer says, "a few valves are leaking, sir. I can fix that. There's no other internal damage apparent and any structural damage to the hull will have to be assessed when we surface."

"Take us down to two hundred meters," Heineke commands the helmsman. He then confides to his number one, "Let's see what depth his charges are set for, Hans."

The next pass by the destroyer is a brutal one. The charges explode much closer to the U-boat. Sea water spurts from leaking valves and some pipe joints throughout the boat. Reports indicate that two of the empty torpedo tubes in the bow and a ballast tank are damaged.

While the boat takes a pounding for four minutes, anxiety levels rise among the crew, but there's no panic. Their apparent bravado during the pummeling by the depth charges is exposed only by the expression of fear in their eyes. Those in the control room look toward their captain, hoping for an order that will cease the explosions that come so close that a direct hit is inevitable during the next volley of depth charges.

The order came. "Helmsman, take us down to two hundred sixty meters."

Hans Topp's eyes roll back in his head for a moment before they return to center and catch the captain's with a stare that shows concern. A recent hull modification to the U-boat has increased the crush depth to two hundred and fifty meters. "Will the pressure at two hundred and sixty meters be too much, Captain?"

Karl Heineke shakes his head, to ease the concern of his exec. "It's okay, Hans, the design engineers have left some margin beyond hull crush pressure. I want to see if the American destroyer has set its depth charges to detonate as deep as two hundred sixty meters."

As the U-boat dives deeper, all eyes in the control room go to the depth gauge…two hundred twenty-five meters…two hundred forty. Metallic clanking and groaning is heard as water pressure squeezes the U-boat. The depth gauge reads: two hundred forty-five…then two hundred fifty.

"Helmsman, level at two hundred and fifty meters before going any deeper." Heineke orders. "We'll wait there for three minutes." He listens to the increase in pressure-related noises as the U-boat hull screams and groans like a human in pain, but no severe damage is reported.

"Helmsman, go to two hundred and fifty-five meters and then hold at two hundred and sixty." Heineke looks at Hans, who appears to be holding his breath, with a wry smile.

The engineer reports: "Captain, there's some minor leaks that I've brought under control with improvised repair action."

Fritz, the radioman reports: "Sir, the propeller sounds of the destroyer indicate it's closing fast toward us at two hundred meters."

The crew braces for another depth charge onslaught, and it comes at them in a volley of explosions spaced six seconds apart. But the turbulence caused by each is less than before.

The engineer reports: "All problems from pressure are minor and now stabilized, sir."

Heineke says to Hans, who is breathing normally again, "Okay, we'll stay at two hundred sixty meters for a while."

The destroyer makes two more passes with its depth charges, exploding no nearer than thirty-five meters above the U-boat.

After the destroyer completes its run, Heineke says, "Okay, let's give the destroyer captain and crew an indication that this U-boat has sustained a lethal hit. Load the number-two torpedo tube with the *kit* and launch it."

The *kit* is made up of twenty gallons of diesel oil and assorted trash. When it reaches the surface with its resultant oil slick, flotsam, and jetsam, it could indicate a successful U-boat break-up to the destroyer crew.

After launching the fake debris, Heineke says, "Now we'll wait forty-five minutes and if there's no contact sound from the destroyer approaching for another run, we'll wait another thirty-five minutes more before going to periscope depth."

With the U-boat at thirty meters, the periscope goes up and breaks through the surface. Heineke searches the horizon for three hundred and sixty degrees. The ocean is clear of any menacing ships, so they surface. The hatch opens and Heineke, Hans, the boatswain's mate, and the chief engineer scurry up the ladder and out into the cold but very welcome fresh air that rides in on a breeze off the Atlantic Ocean. Each man on deck lifts his binoculars and looks around for any destroyers. After finding none, the captain's order is shouted down through the hatch:

"Set a course for Lorient, France." That order brings a resounding cheer from below.

Turning toward Hans, Heineke says, "I won't get you home for Christmas, but before the new year, for sure."

* * *

The U-432 is cruising on the surface at eighteen knots, on a heading toward France. The deck watch crew is in place, and Heineke leaves Hans in charge and goes below. He studies their position at the chart table, estimating they'll make port in Lorient on December 29.

After, in the captain's nook, he changes his shirt, still wet from sweating out the depth charges. He pulls on a gray turtleneck sweater and then glances at Marie Paul's picture. "We've survived another close one. Maybe I'll be with you in Paris for the new year."

Karl Heineke lies on his bunk for the first time in twenty hours and a thought comes to his tired mind. *Now that the Americans are in it, how many more of these onslaughts will we survive?*

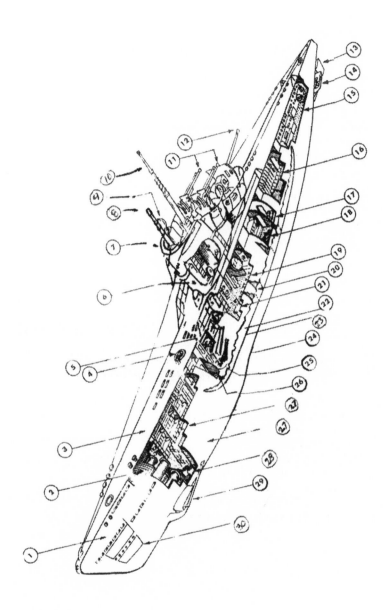

Atlantic U-boat, Type VII, World War II

1. Superstructure
2. Pressure hull
3. Main deck
4. Forward hatch
5. Officers' quarters
6. Tower compartment
7. Bridge
8. Sky periscope
9. Direction finder
10. Attack periscope
11. Anti-aircraft guns (2 cm.)
12. Anti-aircraft guns (3.7 cm.)
13. Rudder
14. Rear hydroplanes and twin screws
15. Motor room and aft torpedo tube
16. Diesel room
17. Galley and washroom
18. Petty officers' quarters and Battery I below deck
19. Control room and rear bulkhead
20. Saddle tank (fuel oil and ballast tanks)
21. Control room and forward bulkhead
22. Radio and sound rooms
23. Captain's nook
24. Battery II below deck
25. Chief Warrant Officers' quarters
26. Forward washroom
27. Bow compartment and men's quarters
28. Four torpedo tubes and spare torpedoes below deck
29. Forward hydroplanes
30. Outer torpedo tube doors

CHAPTER 2

East Bay, Cape Cod, Massachusetts

It's December 20, 1941. America is at war. It's a Saturday afternoon, thirteen days after the Japanese attacked Pearl Harbor…nine days after Germany and Italy declared war upon the United States.

The three boys are at the movies, slouched down in their seats, chewing on Baby Ruth candy bars offered free with a Buck Rogers comic book. The previews are running on the silver screen and they'll be followed by the *Eyes and Ears of Pathe News*, then the weekly *Tarzan* serial, and finally the full-length double feature—all that entertainment for only twenty-six cents.

With the news comes a cloud of smoke over Pearl Harbor, Hawaii. The boys watch the panic and confusion on the faces of the people as they scurry around in the aftermath of a surprise attack by waves of Japanese aircraft.

Junie is fourteen years old. He's taller than the other two by a couple of inches, and has curly black hair and sharp features, including a rather pointed nose. He wears round wire-rim eyeglasses. Junie has a studious look and in fact he's the best student of the three. The other two boys look to him for leadership and he accepts that roll.

Allie, with his oval face, looks a little like a cherub in one of Michelangelo's paintings. He's fourteen. His eyes are brown and his hair is cut short in the wiffle style of the time, the same as Iggy's. Allie is the cautious one, making sure of every step before he takes it.

Iggy is thirteen, but will turn fourteen in April. He has red hair and freckles so thick on his face that they're clustered together in places. At first glance, his large blue eyes are noticed before the freckles or red hair. Iggy's first name was thankfully shortened from Ignatius by his friends. In full, it's Ignatius Peter Broderick. His dad is a third-generation fisherman and Iggy was named after him and his grandfather. Iggy is more serious than the other two and because of that he sometimes bears the brunt of their frivolity.

Nicknames prevail among these teenagers. Junie's real name is Earnest Francis Cohen, the same as his dad, who is a career officer in the Army infantry, stationed on the island of Corregidor. Allie is Allison Raymond Sheffield. His father is the only medical doctor treating the two thousand six hundred and three full-time residents of East Bay. Allie's siblings are his brother, a Navy pilot, and a sister, who's a senior at Boston College.

Allie whispers to Junie, "Those sneaky Japanese sure hit hard. Wonder where they'll drop their bombs next."

"Hawaii is far away from here, so don't worry about Cape Cod," Junie whispers back.

Iggy chimes in, "My brother Larry had his seventeenth birthday a week ago and went off to Boston to join the Marines."

"It's scary," Allie says. "My brother Danny leaves Weymouth Air Station in a few weeks for carrier duty in the Pacific."

"Hey, Allie, watch it!" Iggy quotes a slogan posted in the theater lobby: *A Slip of the Lip Can Sink a Ship*. It could be your brother's carrier."

Allie looks around the theater at the people sitting close to them. He sees Alice Trimble, a third grader, and old Mrs. Perkins, in her eighties. "Yeah, sure, Iggy, Japanese spies are all around us."

"Yeah, but..." Iggy's comeback is interrupted by Junie.

Junie takes his last bite from the Baby Ruth bar, adjusts his glasses to a point higher up on his nose, and says, "My mom says now that Germany is our enemy, too, every guy in East Bay between seventeen and thirty will join or be drafted if they're not already in it, like my dad. A year ago, he was sent to an island in the Pacific called Corregidor." He slaps his rolled-up Buck Rogers comic book on a knee. "No Army infantry for me. No, sir. Soon as I'm seventeen, it'll be the Army Air Corps."

Iggy speaks above a whisper. "When I get to be seventeen, I'm off to join the Marine Corps."

Allie is about to voice his choice of the Coast Guard when an usher comes down the aisle. His flashlight beam shines on each of their faces. "You're out of here if you guys don't quiet down."

They slouch further down in their seats and become quiet as they watch Tarzan fly through the jungle from tree to tree, followed closely by his significant other, Jane.

CHAPTER 3

"Raymond, we have to talk."

"Do we have a problem, Lois?"

It's early on Saturday afternoon and Doctor Sheffield, Allie's father, is in his office with Lois Cohen, Junie's mother-his nurse. Their last patient of the day has just left.

"I feel so guilty about what's going on between us. With Earnest being on that Island of Corregidor fighting the Japanese and your wife, Barbara, in the same house…well, it's shameful and yet I can't stop doing it."

The doctor leaves his desk and takes Lois in his arms saying, "we've gone through this before." He holds her in a tight embrace. "You were lonely…I was lonely. That's how it all started and now it's developed into more than that. It's not a fling at make believe love, it's the real thing. I want to be with you forever and I just need some time to work that out."

"I feel the same love for you and believe you want to leave Barbara, Raymond, but I could not tell Earnest I want a divorce because of the horrid circumstances he's in. That would be cruel. Damn this war!"

"If it wasn't for the war, Lois, our love affair would've never happened."

Their kiss is long and the mounting passion of it transcends any of Lois Cohen's guilty feelings. The doctor removes the two barrettes holding her upswept auburn hair. The long tresses tumble down below her shoulders as he takes her hand and she follows him…again.

17

CHAPTER 4

After the last of the double features ends, the three boys leave the lobby and turn right on East Bay's Main Street in the town center. East Bay, on Cape Cod, Massachusetts, is located on a narrow strip of land that curves seventy miles out to sea from the canal separating it from the mainland. The cold, rough Atlantic Ocean is on one side of the town with the warmer and calmer waters of Cape Cod Bay on the other. East Bay's permanent population of two thousand six hundred and three would normally swell to over three thousand five hundred in pre-war July and August. The full-time residents are mostly fishermen, farmers, and those who support the tourist trade in normal times. But now with the war coming, a period of abnormal time in East Bay has commenced.

They walk along together on Main Street before each will separate and head for their homes. Christmas lights adorn Woolworth's Five & Ten and other stores on the street. A few large snowflakes are falling, but they disappear when touching the ground. A white Christmas is common in Boston, to the north, but a rarity on the Cape.

The three make plans to meet in the morning at the *dune*. It's their special place on the beach, near Highland Light House. It could be their last outing there until March. December is still relatively mild on Cape Cod, but in January and February a winter wind could come off the Atlantic Ocean waters and bring a wet, cold chill to the shoreline.

Junie Cohen leaves the other two after slapping each on the back and saying, "See ya at the dune." He runs up a walkway imbedded in slabs of gray slate and enters the front door of a large Victorian house.

"Hey, Mom, I'm home."

When Junie doesn't get a response from his mother, he starts a search around the house until he finds her in her bedroom. She's sobbing softly.

"Mom, what's the matter?"

"It's your father." A deep sob interrupts her next words. "The island of Corregidor is expected to fall to the Japanese."

"How do you know that?"

She dabs at her eyes with an embroidered handkerchief and looks up at her son. "An Army friend of ours who works in Washington called me this afternoon."

Unknown to Junie, Lois Cohen's sobs are not influenced as much by the danger to her husband as they are by the guilt of her infidelity.

* * *

Allie Sheffield leaves Iggy Broderick further down Main Street. He turns onto Shore Road and, after four hundred yards, trots up a paved driveway and enters a twelve-room colonial that's the oldest house in East Bay. His dad, Dr. Raymond Sheffield, occupies three rooms separated from the living quarters, consisting of a reception area, his office, and an examining room. Lois Cohen, Junie's mother, is his nurse and administrator. She's off at two on Saturday afternoon.

The doctor is sitting at his desk, writing on a chart, when Allie pokes his head in the doorway. "Hi, Dad."

The doctor's short white beard matches the color of his full head of hair. He takes a puff from his pipe and then places it in an ashtray before sitting up straight and looking up at Allie over horn-rimmed glasses. "How was the movie, son?"

"Good, but there was some scary stuff about the bombing of Pearl Harbor."

"Yes, I saw that Thursday night. Allison, I want to talk to you about some changes to our family now that America is at war."

"You're not going to enlist, Dad?"

Dr. Sheffield chuckles. "Heavens, no, I'm a little too old for that and needed here in East Bay. The Coast Guard authorities have asked that I be on call in case of casualties."

"Casualties…you mean people who get shot or bombed by the Japs or Germans?"

"No, that's not too likely, Allison, but the Coast Guard expects some German submarine activity off Cape Cod shores. There could be casualties brought here if Allied ships are torpedoed."

"Wow, I didn't think the war would be so near to us."

"It could be. Don't worry about that just yet." The doctor picks up his pipe and lights the tobacco in a white bowl that isn't burnt to ash. After a couple of puffs to get the pipe going, he says, "The Coast Guard will be patrolling the beaches of the Cape in force soon. The section from East Bay to Provincetown will be under the command of a Commander Childs, and he'll be based here in East Bay. In fact, he'll be staying in our guest room for as long as need be." The doctor looks at his watch. "He's due to arrive here within the hour."

Allie is thrilled knowing that a Coast Guard officer will be living in their house. When the other kids talk about their choice of a branch of service to join, his is always the Coast Guard. His love of sailing in East Bay Harbor, fishing from the shore, spending his summer days on the beach and in the dune shack is the catalyst for that selection. Sometimes he'd bike to a bluff above the harbor and watch a Coast Guard cutter as it made its way into port. He'd wave at the sailors onboard and they'd wave back.

"Will there be many Coast Guard men stationed here? Where will they stay, Dad?"

"Commander Childs is tasked with finding billets for three hundred men. Most likely they'll be housed in the empty hotels without tourists to fill them now, until permanent quarters can be built out at Highland Light."

"Why aren't the Coast Guard men already here, Dad?"

"Because the war came on so suddenly they're very short of men until more enlistments or the draft provides some that are trained. America has been caught short, Allison, and must sustain a great effort to catch up to the might of the Japanese and Germans."

Later, while Allie is lounging in the den, reading an Archie comic book, the front door chimes sound. He jumps up and rushes to the door, anticipating that it might be Commander Childs. When he opens it, a tall blond man in dress uniform stands on the threshold with his hat tucked under his left arm. The luggage beside his right leg is a blue fold-up B-4 bag.

His smile is broad. "I'm Bill Childs." He extends his right hand.

Allie hesitates before he finds the right response and then shakes the hand offered. "Allison Sheffield, sir, but everyone calls me Allie, 'cept my dad."

Commander Childs says, "And, Allie, just call me Bill. I get enough of the *sir* stuff where I work."

Allie picks up the B-4 bag and leads Bill Childs up a circular staircase and into the guest room.

* * *

After Iggy leaves Allie, he walks toward East Bay Harbor, passing by his cedar-shingled cottage home, weathered gray by salt air and sun. When he reaches the dock, he climbs the ladder to board his dad's boat and enters the cabin of the fifty-four-foot trawler, *Elizabeth Ann*. Ignatius Peter Broderick, Sr., is bent over the chart table. He looks up from his study of the navigation charts.

The elder Broderick is a larger version of his son...same red hair and freckles, but his first name, Ignatius, passed down to him through generations of seafaring Broderick's, has not been shortened to Iggy. He is known as Captain Pete around East Bay.

Pete Broderick graduated from Massachusetts Institute of Technology (MIT) in 1932 with a degree in mechanical engineering. He was employed by a Boston firm for three years until he left the confines of his office cubicle to pursue the occupation of his ancestors: fishing the Atlantic Ocean. He'd worked as a first mate for two years until he scraped up enough money to buy the trawler and name it after his wife.

Iggy is fascinated by the boat: the radio, the compass, and all the winches and other machinery used to spread and retrieve the large nets. In April, when he will be fourteen, his dad promised to take him on fishing trips to the Georges Bank.

Pete Broderick swivels his chair away from the chart table. "Hey, Iggy, movie any good?"

"Yes, sir, but the news reel showed Pearl Harbor being bombed and it made me a little nervous." Iggy looks out at the Atlantic beyond the harbor and asks, "Will something like that happen here?"

"Not likely. Right now the German bombers don't have long-range capability. I'm more worried about their U-boats prowling around our shipping lanes, torpedoing merchant ships off Cape

Cod. The ships come out of New York and head for Halifax to be staged in convoys going to England and Russia."

Always eager to learn about the fishing boat's activities, Iggy asks, "Why were you studying the charts when I came aboard? Are you going out tomorrow?"

"No, some First Naval District officers came on board this morning and they showed me the position of minefields and submarine nets outside Portsmouth, Boston, and New York Harbors, also the patrol routes of the Coast Guard cutters and Navy destroyers so the *Elizabeth Ann* will not fish in those waters."

"Wow, Dad, looks like they're expecting some stuff to happen around here."

"Could be, but that's not all." Pete Broderick's glance goes to the radio. "They put a crystal in my radio so I can report the sighting of any enemy submarines to them on a special frequency."

Iggy's large blue eyes open wide as he stares at his dad with an expression that is a mix of fear, excitement, and adventure.

"Okay, enough war talk. Your mom has prepared her special beef stew for us. Let's get on home."

They leave the dock and walk up Shore Road toward the weathered gray house that'd been passed on through three generations of Broderick fishermen. On the way, Antonio Posada, a clam digger and part-time crewmember on the *Elizabeth Ann*, stops his pickup next to them. It's loaded with small buckets of sand.

"Afternoon, Captain and Iggy," Antonio says.

"Hey, Antonio, what's with all the sand pails?"

"An Army guy asked me to fill them with beach sand, Captain Pete, and take them around to houses in East Bay. I'm helping the war effort."

"How's that?" Pete asks.

"Guy says they're for folks to throw sand on any fire started by incendiary bombs dropped on houses in East Bay."

Hearing that, Iggy's previous feelings of excitement and adventure are overtaken by fear.

They take their two buckets of sand from the back of Antonio's truck and enter the cottage to the welcoming smell coming from the kitchen. It is Elizabeth Ann Broderick's beef stew simmering on the wood stove—a delightful respite from the many seafood meals that have graced the Brodericks' table.

Elizabeth Ann is sitting at the dining room table, sewing on some black drapes. "Hello, men. Are you hungry?"

"That we are," Pete answers. He picks up a drape and asks, "What's with all this black cloth you're working on, Elizabeth?"

"They're black-out curtains to cover our windows. The air raid warden, old Charlie Davis, came by with the material and said it's the law that no light should escape our house at night. Something about the light helping German bombers find their targets."

"Maybe submarines could see the lights of East Bay, but I doubt if bombers can make it here from Germany," Pete offers again.

Elizabeth finishes the hem on her last black curtain and, on her way to the kitchen, says, "Charlie told me that all the cars must have headlights painted black halfway from the top. Also, I read in the paper today that gas and food rationing will start soon."

Pete Broderick's eyes follow his wife as she enters the kitchen. His thought is: *The atmosphere of America at war is creeping in like a fog bank to settle over the town of East Bay.*

The Dune

CHAPTER 5

The Dune
Sunday, December 21, 1941

As planned, on Sunday at noon, they pedal two miles along Shore Road to a path that ends close to the dune. They hide their bikes in some sumac bushes and run down the path.

It's their special place on the beach. The dune is a bowl-shaped depression thirty yards back from the high-tide mark. Its walls are twelve feet high in places and were formed by a wind-driven tidal surge during the 1938 hurricane. It offers the boys isolation and protection from the wind along this desolate section of the Atlantic shore. The dune would be safe from erosion until another tidal surge, like the one in 1938, comes in to change the shape of this Cape Cod beach.

To climb in and out of their bunker, they made a crude thirteen-rung ladder from scrap lumber. The ladder faces the Atlantic and they sometimes take turns standing on the eighth rung to watch ships pass by. Highland Light is to the right of the dune on a bluff a mile away. The lighthouse casts its bright beam out over the water every five seconds to warn ships away from the peril of rocks close to shore.

In summer, when the blue fish are running, the ladder serves as a lookout post for the tell-tale ripples made by a school of blues chasing their prey in a feeding frenzy. When that happens, the boys grab fishing poles and wade up to their knees in the surf to cast sea worm-baited hooks out into the midst of that action.

The dune is furnished with three rickety beach chairs. One wooden orange crate is used to store mustard, relish, catsup, and a few canned goods. The other one holds comic books and some serious reading. One book there is a medical dictionary cast away by Dr. Sheffield and confiscated by Allie. In the center of the dune, a grate over some rocks serves to roast marshmallows and potatoes. Sometimes a feast of hot dogs would be their fare. A special treat is freshly caught blue fish smeared with catsup and mustard to absorb the oil...wrapped in foil and then grilled over charcoal. On December days such as this, when a slight chill is in the air, the charcoal glows to warm their dune. When they leave their hideaway, the fire is extinguished with a few handfuls of sand. A tarpaulin made from an old tent is then placed over all their creature comforts.

Junie climbs down the ladder and Iggy follows. They remove the tarp and fold it. Allie tosses the bag of the day's treats to Junie before he climbs down. The bag holds three Cokes, hot dogs, rolls, and three whoopee pies.

They start the charcoal burning under the grate before climbing the ladder for their customary stroll of the beachfront beside the breaking surf. For this December day, the temperature is mild at fifty degrees with a light on-shore breeze.

They're quiet at first, each into their own thoughts while scaling flat rocks and seashells to compete for the most skips over the water's surface. It's a heady time for them as they feel the effect of the country being at war.

Iggy breaks the silence. "Wonder what Christmas will be like this year."

"We'll miss my dad, but that's not all of it," Junie says. "My mom's upset and crying all the time about what might happen on Corregidor, where he's stationed."

"What's happening there, Junie?" Allie asks.

"The Japs may take it over and my dad could be made prisoner or killed."

"Geez, that is bad," Iggy says. "My mom cried when my brother Larry told her the Marines wouldn't let him come home from boot camp for Christmas."

Allie throws a rock that skips over the water six times before breaking some news. "A Coast Guard commander who's in charge of this beach from Orleans to P-Town is staying at my house. He'll be here for Christmas because he's from California."

"Wow! Get to know him. We still want to use our dune. My dad says they may close off the beach to civilians," Iggy adds.

"Yeah, he seems like a good guy." Allie smiles and then releases some other news. "My brother Danny called this morning from Weymouth Naval Air Station. He'll be home for Christmas before he ships out for carrier duty."

"Man, that's what I want to do…fly fighter planes," Junie says as they turn back toward their dune and Highland Light in the distance.

"Hey, guys, wait…that's not all about Danny." He grabs a shoulder of each of them and they stop walking. Allie blurts it out, showing the excitement he feels. "Danny promised me he'd buzz the dune this afternoon on his way back to Weymouth from gunnery practice at sea."

Both Iggy and Junie share Ally's excitement about the fly-by with shriek yells as they run along the beach and then climb down the ladder into the dune.

* * *

Later, they place hot dogs on the grate above glowing coals and each plunk down on the sun-bleached canvas beach chairs. Junie gets up a couple of times to turn the franks. When they're cooked, he forks each into a roll then slathers on catsup, relish, and mustard before handing them to his friends. They lie back in the chairs, sipping on Cokes and savoring each bite of their hot dogs while looking up at the sky. The deep blue color contrasts with several white lines from vapor trails moving eastward high over the Atlantic.

"I'll bet some of those white streaks in the sky are from B-17 bombers headed for England." Junie says. "They'll probably be bombing Germany soon."

"Yeah, they asked for it. I read in the *Boston Traveler* newspaper that the Germans are bombing London every night." Iggy says, before taking a bite out of his whoopee pie and a swallow from the Coke to wash it down.

Allie has finished eating and is up on the ladder, looking out to sea, watching for his brother's Wild Cat fighter plane to appear. When he sees a speck in the sky on the horizon, he's sure it's his brother's plane coming straight at them. He alerts the others and they scramble up the ladder and run out on the beach with their eyes glued on the approaching plane. Then all of a sudden another fighter flies very low and fast over the surf in front of them. It roars by with wings wiggling a greeting before climbing straight up in a twisting spiral to join its wingman. Allie falls back and jolts Junie into Iggy and all three fall to the sand startled and surprised. They'd been intent on watching the decoy plane when Danny Sheffield's F4F fighter popped up near Highland Light and flew low and fast over the surf in front of them.

CHAPTER 6

East Bay, Christmas Day, 1941,

At the Sheffield's home, two sections are added to the dining room table. A red and green tablecloth covers the maple surface. The large roast beef in the center is surrounded by bowls of mashed potatoes, carrots, peas, squash, and turnip. A tureen holds rich, dark gravy, the pride of Barbara Sheffield's culinary skills. Two small dishes contain a brilliant red sauce made from cranberries harvested from a Cape Cod bog.

Doctor Sheffield sits at the head of the table. His wife, Barbara, is at the other end, near the kitchen. At thirty-nine, Barbara is known as "a good-looking woman" by the men and some of the women of East Bay. She is tall at five-seven with a beguiling presence. Her brown hair, high cheekbones and large hazel eyes complement a lithe body, not altered much by age. She was eighteen years old when she became pregnant with Danny and married twenty-eight-year- old Doctor Sheffield. She was in her first year of nurse's training at a Boston hospital, and in accordance with the school rules, her training was over. Barbara had buried the resentment deep inside of having to leave that nursing career and marry so young.

Lois Cohen sits to the doctor's left. Allie had suggested she and Junie be invited after Junie had told him about his dad on Corregidor and how upset his mom was. Bill Childs sits to the doctor's right in his Coast Guard uniform. Next to him is Jane Sheffield, home from Boston College for Christmas. She's a tall brunette who, at twenty, carries the good looks of her mother. When the handsome Coast Guard commander speaks to her, a slight blush paints

Jane's cheeks. Allie thinks he knows the reason for his sister's blushing. He'd overheard his mom and her discussing the merits of the Coast Guard bachelor. During Allie's eavesdropping, Jane was heard to say, "He's gorgeous." And he heard his mother remark: "Yes, I've noticed."

Danny is seated between Jane and his mother. He wears his favorite plaid shirt tucked into a pair of uniform khaki pants. It's a reprieve from the regulation dress of Weymouth Naval Air Station. Allie and Junie are sitting across from him.

"You scared me yesterday, Danny, when you flew around Highland Light and low over the surf in front of us. I was watching the other Grumman F4F when you zoomed by."

Danny grins. "Yeah, Junie, that was my plan."

Allie cups his hand over his mouth and whispers to his friend, "Yeah, Junie, you almost pissed your pants."

The boys giggle until Barbara Sheffield gives them a stern look to quiet them. Then she speaks to her older son. "Danny, I wish you wouldn't fly your plane so low and fast."

Lt. Danny Sheffield grins sheepishly, turns his head to his mother, and nods. "Okay, Mom, I'll be careful." Then he thinks about the kind of flying he'll soon be doing off a carrier in the Pacific.

Doctor Raymond Sheffield, from his command position at the table head, says, "A prayer before we start this feast." He bows his head and the others follow suit. "On this Christmas and at the start of another world war, we pray that all those sent out in harm's way will be made safe." Then he stares at Bill Childs for too long... Bill Childs thinks it's a stare that discounts him from one of those in harm's way. *Maybe I'm reading into it wrongly and I'm oversensitive about not being in combat.*

Lois Cohen starts to sob. The doctor reaches out and grasps her arm. It's a gesture that his wife, Barbara, thinks is beyond a touch. But more than that, it's the way their eyes meet and linger even longer.

The doctor then lifts his glass of red wine. "To this great feast…enjoy the food, for the rationing by our government is about to commence."

The adults and Jane Sheffield raise their glasses of wine while Junie and Allie follow by lifting their Cokes in a mock, non-alcoholic toast. Everyone seated at the table has their own thoughts about what the war will bring before the Christmas of 1942 arrives.

* * *

Inside the gray cedar-shingled Broderick cottage, the Christmas feast and setting is different from that at the Sheffield's. A thick pine harvest table has green placemats at each setting. Thick pine planks on both sides of the table serve as benches for seating and they match the table's varnished and pine-knotted surface. A large red candle glows in the center of the table with sprigs of holly spread near its holder.

The appetizers have been brought by their guests, Antonio and Gina Posada. Antonio had dug a dozen quahogs from the tidal flats that morning. Gina had removed the meat from within each shell and ground it. She then added breadcrumbs, mashed potato, and special spices before stuffing the meat back into the shells. She baked the filled shells in the oven until a brown crust was formed on the surface and then sprinkled each with paprika.

The women serve the quahogs to Pete, Antonio, and Iggy, and then return to the kitchen to fuss over the main course and the accompanying dishes. The men eat the quahog mix and drink Nar-ragansett beer that they pour into their glasses from a quart bottle. Iggy munches away at the quahog mix forked from its shell while sipping on his Coke. He listens to his dad and Antonio talk of fishing and clam digging. The topic centers on the war-time restrictions placed on those enterprises.

"I wonder if the Coast Guard will allow clam digging on the flats," Antonio says. "If they cut that, I'll go broke."

"Yeah, the area I can fish in has been limited by the First Naval District." Pete forks a mouthful of quahog from the shell and takes a sip of beer. "I got a visit from the Navy. Three officers came on board the *Elizabeth Ann* the other day and showed me the restricted areas for fishing boats on my charts."

Antonio grins and says, "Hey, Captain Pete, if we can't make a living here, we'll end up as welders at the Fore River Shipyard."

"No way, Antonio, I couldn't stand being captive in a job like that. I've been there." Pete reaches for another quahog. "On that visit to the *Elizabeth Ann*, the Navy asked me to report any German submarines. They installed a crystal in my radio for a special frequency."

"No shit?" Antonio looks over at Iggy and then says, "Sorry."

"Yeah, things are changing, my friend." Pete turns away from Iggy and whispers to Antonio, "America isn't ready for this war. Not enough men, ships, or planes to patrol the ocean around here."

"Hey, the Navy and Coast Guard gotta eat. So I'll dig clams and you'll fish. Right?"

Pete smiles at his friend. "That's true." Then his expression turns serious. "You know, my son, Larry, was my mate on board the *Elizabeth Ann* before he joined the Marines. I could use you full-time now, Antonio. Okay?"

Antonio thinks about the offer for a couple of seconds. "I can do that. I'll dig clams when we're not fishing and my brother Sal will cover for me when we're out."

Pete reaches for Antonio's hand and gives it a hard shake.

Out in the kitchen, Elizabeth Ann is stirring a kettle containing the meat that'd been shucked from eight boiled lobsters hauled from Antonio's brother Sal's lobster traps in East Bay Harbor. She is making a creamy lobster stew intended for their Christmas dinner's first course. Elizabeth chats with Gina Posada about their sons and some East Bay gossip items. Gina calls Elizabeth Ann "Betty," like everyone in East Bay does except for her husband, Pete.

"You know, Betty, Marcello is my only son and I worry about him being in the Army during this damn war." Tears fill her eyes before she continues. "He was sent to Galveston, Texas for training. His letters hint that he'll be fighting Germans in..." a sob stops her next word.

Elizabeth Ann places the lobster stew on the back of the wood stove to simmer. She takes a bottle of sherry from a cupboard and mixes four tablespoons of it into the stew. Then she sprinkles in a few pinches of paprika. After, she takes two small glasses from the same cupboard and pours the sherry into each. Before handing a glass to Gina, she gives her a hug and says, "My Larry joined the Marines two weeks ago. He's at Cherry Point, North Carolina, in boot training. I feel the same as you, Gina. I'm afraid for him."

Two glasses of sherry help to ease their fears while tending to the main course in the oven and the other food cooking on the stove. Some town gossip also takes them away from worry.

"Gina, have you seen the Coast Guard officer staying at the Sheffield house?"

"Oh, yes, I met him in the drug store. He's very handsome."

"Barbara Sheffield introduced me to him," Elizabeth says. "He's from California and single. Looks to be in his mid-thirties."

"You know... in many ways this war is bringing with it the atmosphere for fast friendships among the lonely. Some of our women whose husbands are away at war have sought male companionship to offset that loneliness. The routine of this small town has changed, Gina, and with it comes temptation."

"Another thing, Gina...the doctor seems to have a thing for Lois Cohen and I think it's more than a working relationship. Her husband has been overseas for a year now and she's with the doctor in his office almost every day. Lord knows what goes on when they're alone there. Also, I've seen them at the Oyster Shack having lunch."

"Well, I know she's upset about Ernest being on that Island of Corregidor surrounded by Japs. Maybe it's just a strong working relationship that they have or something like that."

"Or something like that, Gina. Okay, enough town gossip. Let's serve the Christmas dinner."

Gina ladles the lobster stew into each bowl. Elizabeth Ann checks on the main course baking in the oven and its sauce simmering on the stove. She then calls the men and Iggy to the table and sits down beside her husband.

Before dipping his spoon into the stew, Pete Broderick raises his glass and says, "Here's to Larry and Marcello and all the young men who serve. May they stay safe and be home soon."

After the lobster stew is finished, Elizabeth Ann leaves the table and returns with the main course. It is a large halibut resting on a blue platter that had been brought over from Ireland and passed on through generations of Brodericks. She serves each plate and Gina follows her, spooning out a creamy white sauce on each portion. Then the coleslaw, small boiled potatoes, beets, and carrots are passed around the table.

Iggy looks at the large white fish and says, "Wow, Dad, where'd you get it?"

"Georges Bank, son…it weighed out of the water at twenty-six pounds."

"Is that where you're going to take me for my birthday in April, Dad?"

"That's what I promised."

Elizabeth Ann Broderick looks over at her husband, and Pete knows what her expression says. The North Atlantic is not safe water with the threat of German subs. She has concerns about her youngest son, Ignatius, being out there.

Footnote: Gina Posada's recipe for stuffed quahogs may be found in appendix B

CHAPTER 7

The U-boat is on the surface to charge its batteries. Karl Heineke and Hans Topp are on deck along with the boatswain's mate. The ocean is boiling in a storm with twenty-foot waves breaking over the bow. Visibility is only about one hundred meters so there's no need to scan the horizon with their binoculars. Each wave leaves a spray of cold sea-water on the men as it hits the bow. Conversation is at scream level. The boatswain's mate yells a request for permission to go below to assist the cook with the Christmas dinner. Permission is granted by the captain.

Captain Heineke cups his hands around his mouth and yells, "Merry Christmas, Hans." Hans can only nod his acknowledgment as he braces himself against another wave washing over the deck.

The storm becomes worse and Heineke is about to decide on securing the deck watch when the boatswain's mate opens the hatch, climbs on deck, and makes his way along the roped rail to his captain.

"Sir, the men below are being thrown around and some are seasick. Some equipment has come loose and they're trying to secure it. It's bad below, sir."

Heineke doesn't hesitate. "Clear the deck."

They scramble down the ladder and secure the hatch. The captain views the storm's internal impact from bow to stern. It's even worse than when they were being battered by depth charges.

"Engineer are the batteries charged." Heineke asks.

"Yes sir, all are fully charged."

"Okay, then blow the ballast tanks."

"Helmsman, take us down to forty meters and level there. Stay on course for Lorient."

As soon as they reach a depth of forty meters, the U-boat stops being thrashed by the storm above them. The smooth going is a relief to all and tidying up of boat and crew commences. Some crewmembers have incurred minor cuts and bruises during the boat's foray with the North Atlantic. When the cleanup is over and the minor injuries treated, the Christmas spirit starts to spread through the boat.

"Okay, Hans, we'll stay cruising submerged at forty meters until we're out of this storm. Our speed is only eight knots submerged until the ocean quiets down. That may make us a day late, but I'll still get you to port and on your way to Augsburg before New Year's."

* * *

The cook has done his best with the remaining provisions. He simmers a stew using beef stock, sausage, carrots, and potatoes then seasons it with pepper, salt, and other spices. Hans Topp's contribution to the Christmas feast is five bottles of cognac—a clandestine offering brought on board against regulations while his captain looked the other way. Each crewmember holds his mug out toward Hans and he pours a ration in each one.

The stew is served. They gather in and around the control room after the meal. The last of Hans Topp's Christmas libation is poured. A relaxed atmosphere of informality comes to this band of brother submariners who survived a recent depth charge attack and the wrath of a North Atlantic storm still raging forty meters above them. The U-boat's smooth traverse under the waves adds to their tranquility. Christmas carols are sung.

Heineke comments at the end of Silent Night. "You submariners sound pretty good, but don't expect to be recruited by the Navy choir."

Hans Topp who carried the bass in each carol sung makes a deep down belly laugh and says, "Too bad the rest of you can't carry a tune."

The engineer says, "In all due respect, Number One, it could be that we don't have a belly like yours to resonate the proper sound."

The crew's laughter over that remark reverberates throughout the submarine until the mood is changed to one more solemn by the captain.

Heineke raises his hand to get the crew's attention. "Men, at this time I'd like to offer a short prayer. I pray that we all live through this war to spend future Christmases with our families and loved ones...and may those family members and loved ones remain safe from the bombs that are now falling on Germany."

The crew is silent for a few minutes with thoughts about their captain's prayer as it related to their own survival and that of their loved ones back home in Germany. The silence is interrupted by a young seaman making his first patrol.

"Sir, being a man of the sea myself, I feel bad after we torpedo a ship and leave survivors in the water with no chance of rescue. Wouldn't it be the right thing if we picked some of them up?"

The question brings a few groans from U-432 veterans of the many patrols and ship-sinking actions.

"Men, Seaman Mueller has asked a thoughtful question," Heineke retorts. "We all feel pangs of guilt when survivors are left to flounder in the ocean after we torpedo a ship. This war we've declared on the enemy is a hard and cruel one, which they've answered in kind. They're bombing our cities in Germany, killing women and children as I speak."

"Sir, is there an order prohibiting rescue?" Seaman Meyer asks.

"Yes. Admiral Dönitz has ordered his U-boat commanders not to participate in rescue operations. First off, there isn't room to accommodate prisoners on our boats. Furthermore, a U-boat is in danger of attack by fast-moving aircraft during a rescue with no time to crash dive. For the safety of this crew and boat, while captain of U-432, I will not conduct rescue operations involving survivors from torpedoed ships."

Heineke glances at his watch. "We have another two hours to run under the storm before we must surface for charging. All you men not at a duty station go get some rest so you'll be bright-eyed and sharp for our docking ceremony at Lorient."

CHAPTER 8

East Bay, December 30, 1941,

Coast Guard Commander Bill Childs has just picked up his mail at the post office on Main Street when he sees her. He knows that it's Barbara Sheffield even though his glance catches only the back of her long, form-fitting coat. She is standing in a line outside the town hall to sign up for food rationing books.

"Hi, Mrs. Sheffield," he says as he walks up behind her.

His voice sends a tremor through her body and before she turns to greet him, she senses who it is. After spending a day last week showing him around East Bay, she hasn't seen him since, but has wanted to.

"Hello, Bill. My, you've been a busy one…out of the house at dawn and not back until late at night." After saying that, she wishes she hadn't. *Does he think I'm tracking his movements?*

"Yeah, I've been busy setting up a Coast Guard station at Highland Light. We now have Quonset huts for quarters…so I'll be ending your hospitality on January first."

"Oh…well, you've been a fine guest. Allie and I shall miss you. Why don't you join us for a family get-together on New Year's Eve about seven-ish? It can be your going away party as well. The doctor is in Boston at a burn seminar…kind of short notice. He was called there because of the possibility of casualties brought to East Bay from the sea."

"Thanks, I'll be there. Right now, I'm off to a meeting in Provincetown." He looks up at the sky and says, "It's a great day for late December. Think I'll drive my jeep along the beach to get there."

43

Bill smiles and adds, "Why don't you join me? You can shop while I'm at the meeting."

"It's tempting, but I've got to sign up here for rationing books and then get my car lights painted half-black at the gas station."

"I'll be going there again and you've an open invitation for that jeep ride."

"By the way, Bill, Allie and his friends are out at their dune near Highland Light. Stop by and say hello."

"I'll do that. I must talk to those boys. We're so short-handed I may need their help."

Just then Elizabeth Ann Broderick and Gina Posada come out of the town hall. They walk by Barbara and Bill Childs, greet them, and continue down Main Street.

Gina and Elizabeth Ann are two blocks away in front of the five-and-ten when Gina says, "They do make a handsome couple."

"Now, Gina, let's not rush to any conclusions. By the way, did you know that Dr. Sheffield is in Boston at a seminar...and guess who just happens to also be there? Junie Cohen is staying with Ignatius while Lois is away...that's how I know. Do you think I'm just a tongue-wagging East Bay gossip, Gina?"

Gina chuckles. "That could be a better activity than worrying about our sons fighting in this war."

* * *

At the Dune

Junie climbs the ladder, takes a deep breath of the crisp ocean air and says, "It feels real good to be here and away from school during this Christmas and New Year's break."

"Yeah, but us being able to be here in December is the best part," Allie adds."

"Nothing but blue sky...just like the song, guys."

"Please don't sing it, Iggy, just hand me that last marshmallow."

Iggy hands Junie the last marshmallow from a box of them they'd devoured after roasting at the end of sticks held over the charcoal grate until they were a crispy brown. After the boys finish them, they sit in the antiquated, sun-bleached beach chairs, each reading a selection from their orange crate library. Iggy Broderick is absorbed in a Buck Rogers comic book. Allie Sheffield holds a *Big Little Book*. And Junie Cohen is engrossed in the cast-off medical journal that Allie had retrieved from Dr. Sheffield's office.

Allie looks up from his book and speaks to Junie. "Why are you always reading stuff in that medical book? You gonna be a doctor?"

"Hey, there's a lot of stuff in here about women and sex we need to know." He gets up from his beach chair and shows Allie the page he's on. It's a full view of a naked female body with the various parts annotated. Then he whispers to Allie and they both grin. "Let's do the hair on palms thing to Iggy."

A few minutes later, Junie says, "Wow, listen to this. It's all about masturbation."

That word said loudly gets Iggy's attention and he asks, "What's it say, Junie?"

"Okay, I'll read it to you. It says a recent study has shown that frequent masturbation will cause black hairs to grow on the palms of hands."

Allie and Junie look at Iggy on the sly as he coyly turns over both hands to check his palms. They roar with delightful laughter at the deep blush on Iggy's face as he says, "You bastards."

Later, when Junie is standing on a rung of the ladder, looking out toward the ocean, he sees a jeep driving along the beach toward the dune from the direction of Highland Light. As it comes closer he can make out the words printed below the windshield: *UNITED STATES COAST GUARD.*

"Oh, shit!" Junie turns to warn the others down inside the dune. "Here comes the Coast Guard to kick us off the beach."

Allie jumps up from his beach chair and steps up the ladder to a rung below the one on which Junie is standing. By that time the jeep has reached the dune. He recognizes Commander Childs sitting in the passenger seat.

"Hey, guys, relax…it's Bill Childs, the Coast Guard officer I told you about that's staying at our house. Come on, let's see what's up."

They scramble up the ladder and out of the dune to meet the jeep as it pulls up. Bill leaves his seat and walks toward them.

"Hi, Allie…so this is your dune."

"Yes, sir. And I hope we can still use it with the war and all."

"Well, let me take a look, but first introduce me to your friends."

Allie introduces Iggy and Junie formally, without using their nicknames. Childs shakes both of their hands and says, "Please call me Bill." Then he looks down into the dune. "You've got all the comforts of home here."

Junie asks, "Can we stay here on the beach, Bill?"

Commander Childs doesn't answer right away. He looks out to sea and then to his right toward Highland Light and left toward Provincetown. "Yes, you can stay here at your dune, but I'm going to put you to work. I need you boys to patrol a couple of miles of this beach starting at Highland Light. You'll do it on Saturday and Sunday until I can get some more people here to relieve you. Is that okay?"

All three nod their heads in agreement. It's Iggy Broderick who asks what the patrol will involve.

"I want you guys to observe any flashes of gun fire or noise out at sea…report any strange objects or debris washing ashore. The beach will be closed to civilian traffic, so anyone or anything unusual should be reported." He held the eyes of each boy for a few seconds with his own before saying, "You'll be my eyes and ears along this stretch of beach, as well as serving your country. German submarine activity off shore is increasing. I'll supply some binoculars and radios so that you can keep in touch with my beach command post at Highland Light. Any questions?"

There are none. Each boy's broad smile accompanied by a few playful nudges to the ribs express how happy they're to be a part of the war effort.

"Okay, I'll get a patrol schedule to you by this weekend and swear you in." He glances toward the driver in the jeep. "Murphy, bring me those Coast Guard Auxiliary arm bands."

He hands each boy one. "I want each of you to get your parents' permission in writing. If they have any questions, have them contact me."

Junie says, "My mom is in Boston visiting a friend. She won't be home for a couple of days. I'm staying with Iggy. Is that okay?"

"Sure, just get those permissions in to me soon as you can and tell your parents that for the most part, you'll be making patrols on weekends during the day. The three of you will be doing it together with a possible night patrol once in a while on Friday or Saturday."

After Bill Childs's jeep leaves, headed toward Provincetown, Junie says what the others are feeling. "Wow, we keep the dune *and* we're now in the Coast Guard Auxiliary. It can't get much better than that."

"Yeah," Allie says, "but it could get scary on night beach patrols with German subs so near."

"Don't worry," Junie exclaims. "Those U-boats have got to travel a long ways to get to Cape Cod."

Eastern Sea Frontier, December 30, 1941

Enemy Action Diary

2100 An Army ordnance boat en route to Fishers Island from Fort Terry on Plum Island saw a periscope at Lat. 41 degrees 11' 30" Long N. 72 degrees 11'35"W. and had to give hard rudder to avoid ramming it...

CHAPTER 9

Lorient, France, December 30, 1941

As U-*432* approaches Lorient Harbor, the atmosphere on board is thick with celebration. The men look forward to breathing fresh air, eating fresh food, and being free from the confines of a crowded U-boat after fifty-eight days on patrol. They make jokes and chide each other as they put on their dress uniforms in preparation for the formation on deck when the U-*432* docks at its berth among the sub-pens of Lorient.

Karl Heineke is on the bridge with Hans Topp, directing the approach into their assigned pen. Both have shaved off their sixty-day beard growth and have on dress uniforms with medals grouped on their chests. The submarine command staff members, aware of the U-*432's* successful patrol, are lined up on the quay. A sixteen-piece band strikes up a naval marching song as the boat slips into its pen. When the docking is complete, the band plays "Germany Over All."

Hans has mustered the crew into formation on deck, where they stand at attention. A gang plank is lowered and, as it is the custom, a senior staff officer will be piped aboard. To the dismay of Oberleutenant Heineke, that officer is Admiral Dönitz, the commander of submarine operations. The admiral's walk toward Heineke is brisk. He returns the U-*432* captain's salute.

The admiral's speech is short. He puts the crew at ease and says, "I commend this crew of U-*432* for an outstanding patrol, sinking record tonnage." Then a staff officer steps forward and holds out to the admiral an open box lined in purple velvet. Admiral Dönitz reaches inside and grasps its contents. "Oberleutenant Heineke, you have distinguished yourself as a U-boat commander. You and your crew are responsible for a total tonnage of 282,200 in enemy ships sunk in six patrols. For that, I award you the Iron Cross."

The admiral places the medal around Heineke's neck and takes one step back to salute him. The band plays a military march. Karl returns the admiral's salute, in awe of being awarded the esteemed Iron Cross.

The admiral steps close to Karl and speaks in a low voice. "After you dismiss your crew, please report to my office."

After the admiral departs with his staff, Heineke dismisses his crew, and he and Hans are alone on deck.

Hans shakes Karl's hand. "Congratulations, my captain." Then it's a hug for his friend. "An Iron Cross and an invitation to the admiral's office…" Hans smiles and, with a wink, says, "It doesn't get much better than that."

Karl holds the Iron Cross, hanging on a gold chain around his neck, out toward Hans. "Hans, half of this medal belongs to you. The least I can do is authorize ten days' leave and your immediate transport to Augsburg."

"But, Karl, I must remain here to prepare for our next patrol. Don't we start another one in ten days, as usual?"

"Not this time. The staff maintenance officer took a quick look at U-432 and ordered a major inspection and repair with some upgrades." Karl glances at the boat from bow to stern. "The depth charges and Atlantic storm have caused some damage and a new antenna will be mounted along with code changes to *Enigma*. So, enjoy your leave with your family and be back here in two weeks for the loading of fuel, torpedoes, and final provisioning. We sail on January 31… Happy New Year, 1942, Hans."

* * *

Karl enters the admiral's outer office and salutes his adjutant, Kapitanleutnant Godt, who stands from his desk and extends his hand.

"Congratulations, Oberleutnant Heineke, on your award of the Iron Cross. Right this way...the admiral is expecting you."

Karl follows the adjutant down a long, carpeted corridor until they reach Admiral Karl Dönitz's office. Dönitz sits behind a mahogany desk with a large window behind it. The view overlooks the submarine pens and part of Lorient Harbor. His uniform is all white except for the gold braid on its sleeves and the rows of colorful medals on the breast of his tunic. His bearing is straight, if slight, with sharp facial features and thinning white hair combed flat. He rises from his chair and comes around to the front of his desk, where Karl is standing at attention with his white hat tucked under his left arm.

Before Karl can raise his hand in a salute, the admiral's hand reaches his own in a handshake. He then gestures toward a brown leather couch. "Please sit, Heineke."

Admiral Dönitz then speaks to his adjutant, Godt, who is standing by, anticipating his order. "Günter, please see to it that coffee and something stronger gets here."

They sit and Dönitz studies Karl's face for a few seconds before saying, "You know, your father and I served together in the first war. He was my brave captain and friend when I was executive officer aboard U-16."

"Yes, sir. He spoke kindly of you many times. He even named me after you. When he heard you were in command of the submarine fleet, he convinced me to join."

"I'm flattered having that endorsement from Kurt, and having him name his son after me. How's my friend doing?"

"He's struggling with the minor aches and pains of old age and dimming eyesight, but through it all he's determined to serve again."

The admiral chuckles. "Sounds like the Kurt Heineke I know." He then looks straight into Karl's eyes. "The reason I asked you to come here is two-fold. First, I want to hear directly from all my U-boat commanders about their patrols." His search into Karl's eyes becomes more intense. "I want to hear about the real problems so that I may react to correct them. Secondly, I'll brief you on a new operation along the East Coast of America that you'll be involved in."

They drink their coffee, followed by a dram of schnapps. Karl tells of some operational difficulties, including the failure of torpedoes after launch. Then he touches on a subject from scenes burned into his memory that is also an issue bothersome to his crew. "Admiral, when we surface after an action, the vision of a ship's survivors floundering in the water with no hope of rescue is a hard one."

"Yes, I know, Heineke, and I've been bothered by that situation." A sad expression is painted on the admiral's face. "Rescue at sea by submarine is a dangerous action. A crew and U-boat may be lost while engaged in that humanitarian activity." His expression turns from sad to stern. War is hard, Heineke. My order for U-boats not to pick up survivors is the most difficult I've ever made, but it still stands."

After more talk about crew morale and enemy tactics, the admiral terminates the briefing by Karl. "Come with me to the map room."

Karl follows him to a room at the end of the corridor where maps cover all four walls. Dönitz picks up a wooden pointer and moves in front of a large map showing the Eastern seaboard of the United States. He draws his pointer along the coast of Maine and New Hampshire then lingers over Boston, Cape Cod, and Long Island, New York. Then the pointer slides along the Carolinas, ending in the ocean off Florida.

"If we have any chance of winning this war, we must sink ships leaving these ports." The pointer snaps down hard on the harbors of Portsmouth, New Hampshire, Boston, New York City, and the southern port cities. "Ships are leaving these ports to group here." He moves the pointer north to Halifax, Nova Scotia. "From here, ships laden with supplies are staged as convoys and then sail to Russia or England."

Dönitz stares hard at Heineke. "We must get to these ships before they are protected in convoys. Your U-432 will patrol an area from the Gulf of Maine to Cape Cod and Long Island Sound, and south to the Carolinas, with the possibility of being sent to even more Southern waters." His pointer moves to those off-shore ocean regions as he speaks. "This area will be covered by other U-boats." He moves to a wall with the Southern United States map and brushes the pointer over Florida, Texas, and Louisiana shore-lines. "If the activity there is heightened, I may send you South, also."

Karl Heineke studies the map showing his assigned patrol and then asks the admiral, "Sir, how many other U-boats will patrol the area you've assigned me?"

"Seven other boats will join you. All will act as single marauders. My U-boat wolfpacks will continue to attack ships in mid-ocean once the convoys are made up. This operation off the East Coast of America will be known as 'Drumbeat.' We must work fast before the Americans improve their anti-submarine tactics. Any more questions?"

Karl has a few, but hesitates too long.

"Very well...you will coordinate the activities of the other boats in your patrol and report to me in code on *Enigma*."

Admiral Dönitz smiles and shakes Karl's hand. "Help me make Operation Drumbeat such a success that even Hitler will notice."

Then as a closing gesture, he offers, "The maintenance officer has the U-432 for three weeks so you may take leave at our submariners' rest camp in the Alps."

"Sir, if it's okay, I'd rather go to Paris on leave and be back here in two weeks to monitor the progress of repairs, make a trial run, and start provisioning for the Operation Drumbeat patrol."

Dönitz's expression is whimsical. "Of course, of course...Paris for the New Year...the City of Love. Bon voyage, *Kapitanleutenant* Heineke."

With those words from the admiral, Oberleutnant Karl Heineke has just been promoted to kapitanleutnant.

As Heineke reaches the adjutant's desk, Godt stands and hands him the sealed orders for Operation Drumbeat along with documents relating to his promotion. He waits there a few minutes for the hastily typed Paris leave authorization. Godt congratulates Karl and, along with the leave papers, passes him the kapitanleutnant insignias and gold braid to be sewn onto his uniforms.

Karl leaves Submarine Headquarters and walks the main street of Lorient toward the pen where U-432 is berthed. Along the way, he passes by Bistro Luis, where music blares and happy voices of U-boat crews reach the street. He knows the men inside are celebrating making it back alive once again from those long patrols where they'd been under stressful conditions and near death. It's a time to celebrate before going out once again to patrol the cruel ocean inside an iron coffin with depth charge terror raining down on them.

A few steps up the gang plank and he's on board U-432. It's good to be alone there and not have to make his way toward the captain's nook through a bevy of crew and hanging provisions. He sits at the small desk and glances at the picture of Marie Paul. He thinks about her being named after both mother and father, who are farmers in Normandy. He smiles when he remembers teasing her about the masculine part of her name. Then his thoughts stray to when they'd first met in Paris.

The year was 1933 and the world is at peace. I've finished two years at the Sorbonne in Paris, majoring in French and English, and would graduate in 1935. She's twenty; I'm twenty-one. At first, it's a platonic relationship between two students attending the same classes. We share coffee and sandwiches in a brasserie on the Left Bank of the Seine. Soon, we're in love in the city that nurtures romance.

Karl continues to reminisce about her beauty: dark hair, large brown eyes, her well-proportioned body so wanting when they'd made love in the late afternoon in his loft on Boulevard Saint-Germain after classes. Thoughts of that passion stayed with me while at sea and it calls out more loudly to me now in anticipation of my being with her after so long.

I dreaded that time in 1936 when I had to tell her I'd made a decision to follow my father and become a submarine cadet candidate. She was angry, and the angst was more about her hatred of war and those who make it. I attempted to explain that my decision was a practical one based on the premise that a war was soon to come and that I could be drafted into the infantry if I didn't volunteer...and the technology contained within a submarine intrigued me. When I left for cadets, we parted...still deeply in love. All my leave time was spent with Marie Paul in Paris until the war between France and Germany made visits there impossible.

It's been over a year since we've been together. Her letters are rare, having to take a circuitous route to get to me before and after the fall of Paris. Now, Paris is a city occupied by the German Army, making it possible for my visit. It is more complicated for Marie Paul. She'd be ostracized by the Free French if she were known to be fraternizing with a German officer. I'm sensitive to that concern and I'll be careful not to be seen in uniform with Marie Paul by the French Resistance so that the risk of their retaliation against her will be minimized.

My visit will be a surprise since there is no way to get a message about my leave to her on such short notice. Phone lines from Lorient to Paris are inoperative due to a recent English bombing raid. The Sorbonne, where she is an assistant professor, will be closed for New Year's, and travel out of Paris has been restricted by the occupiers, so he's quite sure she'll be at home. I'll go directly from the train station to Boulevard Saint-Germaine and phone her from a close-by brasserie before going to her apartment.

Karl undresses and lies down on his bunk. He plans to leave by train for Paris in the morning. Thoughts of meeting Marie Paul are vivid as he glances at her picture before drifting off to sleep…a sleep not disturbed by his command responsibility in a now silent and safe U-*432*.

CHAPTER 10

East Bay, December 31, 1941

The New Year's Eve dinner at the Sheffield house, hosted by Barbara, consists of only three place settings. The doctor is still in Boston, attending the burn seminar. Jane Sheffield is staying at her college roommate's parents' home in Chatham, and both girls are bringing in 1942 with their dates at a dance hall there…so it's only Barbara, Bill Childs, and Allie who enjoy the roast beef dinner with all the trimmings.

When they finish dessert around nine, Allie has a request. "Mom, Junie Cohen is staying at the Broderick house tonight with Iggy because his mom is in Boston for a couple of days. Can I sleep over there tonight with those guys? It's okay with Mr. and Mrs. Broderick." Allie's look is a pleading one.

Barbara doesn't answer her son right away…she is thinking about the coincidence of Lois Cohen making the trip to Boston at the same time her husband is there. *Too many chance happenings are occurring lately that involve the doctor and his nurse administrator.*

Allie interrupts his mother's thoughts of condemnation. "Well, Mom, can I sleep over with the guys at the Brodericks' house?"

"You may go to the Brodericks' as soon as you clear the table and help with the dishes."

By the expression on Allie's face, Bill can tell that any delay for him to be with his friends is distressful, so he volunteers. "I'll help clean up, Barbara, so Allie can run along."

"But you're a guest, Bill," she protests.

"A guest that just had a great meal. Least I can do."

The thought of the two of them being alone sends a tremor through Barbara's body. "Okay, Allie, off you go. Bring some clean clothes and your toothbrush."

Allie kisses his mom and scampers up the stairs to his room. He leaves soon after.

Before cleaning off the table and doing the dishes, Barbara and Bill sit and talk, sipping what remains of a bottle of a rich red California Merlot that had been sent to Bill by his brother.

"Tell me a little about your life, Barbara."

"Well, here goes. I was eighteen, in my first year of nursing training when it was interrupted."

"What happened?"

"I became pregnant with Danny and the rule was a dismissal from school."

"And you married the doctor."

"Right, and I've always regretted that because I wanted a nursing career."

"Regretted the marriage or not continuing in nursing?"

"My, you do ask questions that probe deep. Well, the honest answer to that is...both. And that frank answer from me deserves some information about Bill Childs."

"Okay, fair enough. I joined the Navy during the start of the Depression. Became an officer and served on a destroyer."

"But you're in the Coast Guard. How did that happen?" She asks.

"I switched to the Coast Guard two years ago because of a chance for promotion there."

"Well, it seems that's gone well for you...being in charge of so many men defending our shores."

Yeah, it's okay. But I have this guilt about not being in combat. Any way, the good part about being stationed here on Cape Cod is meeting you, Barbara." There's a pause before he says... "and Allie."

58

She smiles at that hesitation. "Your duty on the shore of Cape Cod is an important one and so many of your men depend on you." Then, as an afterthought, she laughs and says, "I know some young boys that also depend on you. Allie is thrilled to be in the Auxiliary Coast Guard service."

"Oh, then I have your approval. I really need those kids until more manpower gets trained and assigned to me. This war came on fast and we were not ready for it. I've received Peter Broderick's okay, but I've yet to get permission from Mrs. Cohen."

A dark expression is cast on Barbara's face when she says, "Lois Cohen is in Boston." She looks at her watch. "Oh, my...we've chatted for two hours and it's almost 1942."

* * *

Later, when they are standing close, doing the dishes, that intimacy starts to transcend the task. It peaks for Bill when their hips accidentally touch as he reaches for a dish. And that contact triggers the same excitement within Barbara's body.

She suddenly looks up into his eyes and blurts out, "My husband is having an affair and I don't give a damn."

At first it's a reflex action to comfort her when he takes her in his arms, but it soon becomes much more. It's a short kiss on her neck, and then his lips go to her eyes, where he tastes the salt of a tear. Next it's a long kiss while he helps her probing tongue find his own. Both of their hands explore during the kiss. He finds a button on the side of her dress...she first touches his thigh and then moves her hand upward to find his excitement there. Still in that same embrace, they slip down to the kitchen floor.

CHAPTER 11

Paris, France, December 31, 1941

For Karl Heineke, the train ride from Lorient to Paris is a long one. The warning of an air raid by English bombers sidetracks the train outside of La Mans until it would finally glide into Montparnasse Station four hours late. It is 4:00 p.m. on New Year's Eve.

He leaves the train and walks toward the taxi stand outside, noting that the station along the way is crowded with those wearing German uniforms. It's his first visit since the occupation and he's curious about the changes in Paris caused by the conquerors. There's an elderly French couple in front of him in the queue waiting for a taxi. When it's their turn to enter one, they are held back by the dispatcher, who waves Karl on ahead. Karl speaks to them in polite French and motions for the two to ignore that gesture. The couple shows surprise and thanks him before they proceed into the taxi. The dispatcher shrugs his shoulders and gives Karl a strange look. Karl thinks, *The man is just enacting one of the privileges of a conqueror. And I'm determined not to take advantage of any of those during this visit to Paris.*

The ride toward the Left Bank to a brasserie he knows of on Boulevard Saint-Germain is a pleasant one, for the Paris sights and scenes haven't changed since his peacetime visits. The Eiffel Tower still stands tall and the Arc de Triumph remains to guard the entrance to Avenue Champs Elysees. Except for the German uniforms and military vehicles, it's the Paris of his youth: an everlasting city not yet scarred by a war, a city where his love for Marie Paul had once flamed and would now rekindle.

The taxi drives slowly along Boulevard Saint-Germain. The shops nestled on the first floor of the brownstone buildings are familiar and welcome Karl back with their fond memories as he passes by them: a favorite bakery where students bought long thin loaves of bread for a few coins, the cheese shop, a wine shop, the cafés, the bistros, the brasseries—all open now to serve the occupying German military.

The taxi pulls to the curb in front of the Brasserie Albert at 151 Boulevard Saint-Germain. Marie Paul's apartment is only a block from there and during the Sorbonne student days, they'd spent many hours seated at an alcove window booth sipping coffee while studying and speaking English...and when either received extra money from home, it was the fare of the brasserie accompanied by a carafe of the house red wine. The owner, Albert Chabot, kindly tolerated the long-term occupancy of that alcove booth.

When Karl enters, he's greeted by a man wearing a green leather apron. His hair is white with a beard to match. Seven years have aged Albert Chabot, but his voice of greeting has the same friendly tone Karl remembers. Albert comes forward to assist in the removal of Karl's long leather coat and doesn't seem to recognize him. Karl thinks, *Has this war altered me beyond recognition in just seven years?*

"Welcome to Brasserie Albert..." Albert Chabot pauses while glancing at the insignia showing Karl's rank. "Kapitanleutenant."

"Albert, I'm Karl Heineke. Marie Paul and I..." He gestures toward the booth in the alcove.

"Oh, pardon, pardon...of course, of course." He searches Karl's face for the first time since greeting him. A hug and kiss on both cheeks follow. His eyes move down Karl's uniform. "I never expected you to become a German officer. Perhaps I thought of you still as a student. Marie Paul comes here frequently, but never mentions you. When I asked about you a few years ago, she just shrugged...so I never ask again. Come, we must have a drink for the new year."

He hangs up Karl's coat and leads him past the bar and some tables, where German officers and a few civilians are seated, drinking beer. Karl nods to each of the men as he goes by, hoping that there would be no "heil Hitler" gestures for him to answer in kind. When they're seated in the alcove by the window, Albert summons a waiter and asks, "What will be your pleasure, Karl?"

"I'd like a beer...anything stronger might hit me too hard. I've been on a submarine patrol for a long time and there's a lady by the name of Marie Paul I'd like to bring in the new year with. In fact, I would like to reserve this booth for dinner." He grins at Albert. "I promise that we'll dine and not sip coffee for hours like we did when we were students."

The beer comes with Albert's white wine. Albert raises his glass in a toast. He looks around the room at the German soldiers seated at the bar and at tables. "The year 1940 was a good year for the wine. The grapes of France did not surrender."

Karl leans toward Albert and whispers, "I am not a Nazi. I leave the political ideals to others and concern myself only with getting my crew through this war alive." He raises his beer. "May the war end soon. Has it been rough for you, Albert?"

"Not so bad since the occupation...business is good. My concern is that the Free French may accuse many of us of collaborating with the enemy when the war ends. They will not understand the fine line between survival and collaboration."

Karl takes this opportunity to tell Albert about his concerns. "I will soon telephone Marie Paul and then go to her apartment, but I want to protect her from any of those who may accuse her of aiding and comforting the enemy by being with a German officer."

Albert takes a moment to think of a plan then says, "In the rear of all our restaurants, shops, and apartments on Boulevard Saint-Germain there is an alleyway, and each building has an entrée door there in the back. Mine is in the same hallway as the toilet. We shall deliver your coat to you later. You must leave with the premise of going to the toilet and one of my waiters will escort you to Marie Paul's building along the alleyway away from any of the curious on the boulevard. You may come here tonight the same way. But, Karl...it would be best if you came tonight without a uniform."

"Good, Albert. I'll call her now...and thank you."

Karl enters the public phone booth, deposits some coins, and dials Marie Paul's number. After four rings he starts to worry that his guess about her being at home could be wrong, but on the fifth ring she answers.

"Hello."

Just that one word from a voice he knows so well sends shivers through his body. He speaks to her in English. "Happy New Year, Marie Paul."

He hears a gasp and then, "Karl is it you? Where are you? Oh, my God!"

"I'm in Paris on leave for two weeks and would like to begin 1942 with you. I'm at Brasserie Albert and Albert has a plan for me to get to you without anyone in the shops and on the street noticing."

"So close? Oh, I can't believe this. I was worried when I didn't hear from you for months."

"I was on a long patrol and when I returned to Lorient, the phones to Paris were out."

"Can you come here right now, Karl?"

"Yes, but I want to be careful. I'll be entering through the back of your building in ten minutes."

* * *

Karl opens the door in the back of Marie Paul's apartment building and climbs the two flights of stairs. Her apartment door is ajar. When he enters, she's standing in the foyer waiting for him. He gathers her into his arms and buries his face into her shoulder-length hair. There's the familiar scent of her soap there and it's a warm, welcome memory. The hug that lasts minutes is followed by a long kiss until Marie Paul holds him at arm's length, looks up at his face, and says, "You are much the same. I expected some changes brought on by the war."

"And you, Marie Paul, are now more than beautiful."

They kiss until she pulls away again and her brown eyes travel over his uniform. "A handsome German officer now, not my fellow English student. I shall fix that."

She starts unbuttoning his tunic first and next comes his shirt. When she finishes undoing his belt and the last button of his pants, he has already removed her blouse and bra and his head nuzzles at her breasts, kissing one and then the other. From deep in her chest, Karl hears either a sigh or a sob before she takes his hand and leads him to her bed.

They make love fast and furious the first time, and during the other times it is sensitive and extended. In between, they touch and explore each other's nakedness while talking of their carefree student days, the changes to Paris and the world brought on by war... until their arousal surpasses any further conversation.

They doze and it's Karl whose eyes open first. It takes a moment before he realizes with relief that he's not in the bunk of the captain's nook on board the U-432. He moves toward Marie Paul and kisses her awake. Then with lips close to her ear, he whispers, "Let's celebrate New Year's at Brasserie Albert. I've reserved the alcove booth. Also, I'd like to shed my uniform to protect you from any prying eyes before we go there."

Marie Paul bolts upright on the bed and asks, "Is it dangerous for you to be found out of uniform?"

"Perhaps, but I'll carry my leave orders and military identification and take that risk. Can you find any civilian clothes for me?"

"I have some that my brother André left here when he went…" She pauses, before saying, "to join the Resistance. He is close to your size."

"Good…and your secret about your brother is safe with me."

* * *

They enter the back door of Brasserie Albert and receive a warm greeting from Albert Chabot. Karl is comfortable in his civilian clothes, consisting of slacks, a white shirt, and a brown leather jacket. Albert leads them to the booth in the alcove, where they sit next to each other instead of across.

The tables in the brasserie are filled with New Year's Eve diners. For the most part, they're occupied by German military with their French lady escorts. A six-piece orchestra has set up and is playing a request from the Germans: "Lili Marlene."

Karl orders a carafe of the house merlot. The dark red wine arrives with two glasses just as they finish selecting their choices for dinner from a limited war-time menu. For Karl, it is beefsteak with carrots, beets, and small boiled potatoes. It will be his first red meat in over three months. Marie Paul selects the salmon with the same root vegetables. Karl raises his glass to toast Marie Paul. She's wearing a long-sleeve white blouse with a V-neck. Her dark hair is a vivid contrast to the blouse as it falls loose on her shoulders.

She raises her glass and looks into Karl's eyes. "Let's enjoy these few days together, for we do not know what the rest of this war will bring. And let's speak tonight in English, as in our student days."

After they touch their wine glasses and set them down on the table, Karl turns to her. "I'll always love you." He follows that with a kiss and is holding her hand when the food arrives.

Karl is savoring his first bite of the beefsteak when a murmur from the other tables brings his attention to the brash entrance of an SS officer into the brasserie. The officer has a rank of Oberleutenant and is accompanied by a civilian in a business suit. Both men start going from table to table, checking the identification papers of the French civilians seated there.

Karl whispers to Marie Paul, "The Gestapo has arrived."

They reach the alcove table and, speaking in French, request identification papers from Karl and Marie Paul. Karl stands up and to the tall, heavyset blond officer says, in German, "I am a German officer in the submarine service on leave."

The short Gestapo agent with a thin black mustache has Marie Paul's papers in his hand when he demands Karl's. Karl reaches in the inside pocket of his jacket and hands his identification and leave orders to the SS officer, ignoring the outstretched hand of the civilian. He speaks again to the officer, "This is ridiculous and our food is getting cold." He then says to Marie Paul, speaking in English, their language of the evening, "Can you believe such an interruption to our meal?"

That English phrase spoken by Karl prompts the two men to walk a few steps away and start an animated conversation while glancing at the papers taken from Marie Paul and Karl. Finally, after five minutes of discussion, they return to the table.

"You must come to headquarters with us," the German officer says.

Karl rises from the table again. "This is a mistake." He glares at the SS officer and repeats, "I'm a German naval officer with the rank of Kapitanleutnant. I'm on leave. Why am I being arrested, Oberleutenant?"

The Gestapo agent steps between them. "You are being detained for questioning because you are wearing civilian clothes and speaking in English."

"I gave you my military orders and officer identification. So, I'm in civilian clothes. That's a minor offense to be reported to my commander and handled by him. The lady and I speak English because years ago we studied it at the Sorbonne together. Now, may we finish our meal?"

There is another short discussion between the SS officer and the Gestapo agent before they return to the table. The Gestapo agent says "We've decided that you both must come with us to headquarters for questioning." His upper lip below his mustache curls into a sneer. "We suspect that your papers may be forgeries and you could be foreign agents or members of the French Resistance."

"Wait, why does the lady have to go? Were not her papers in order?" Karl asks.

"Yes, but we must question her also."

The German officer has his hand on his holstered pistol when he asks, "Now, will you come with us quietly?"

* * *

They're driven to Gestapo headquarters and, upon entering the building, Karl is separated from Marie Paul by a female. The matron, who is large with short black hair, grabs Marie Paul roughly by the arm and leads her away while Karl protests.

He's brought to an interrogation room with no windows. It's sparsely furnished with only two straight-back chairs and a desk occupied by a Gestapo agent other than the one who made the arrest. The man at the desk is being shown the papers confiscated from Karl and Marie Paul by the agent with the thin mustache. The arresting Oberleutenant stands at attention next to the desk.

After a few minutes, the man at the desk, who appears to be in charge, looks up at Karl and asks in French, "What have you got to say for yourself?"

Karl answers him in German, wanting to remove any misgivings about his national origin. "I'm a German naval officer of the submarine service stationed, when I'm not at sea, in Lorient, France."

"Why are you not in uniform?" the man behind the desk asks.

The question brings on a sneer from the thin-mustached one.

"I'm guilty of that infraction only." Hoping that fabrication would conceal the real reason, he says, "My dress uniform is in need of cleaning and repairs after months of damp storage at sea on a U-boat."

The Gestapo agent behind the desk looks down at his notes and then jerks his head upward, asking, "Why were you speaking in English to the mademoiselle?"

"We were English-language students at the Sorbonne before the war." Just then Karl's eyes go to the two telephones on the desk. "All this can be cleared by calling my base at Lorient to confirm who I am."

This gets the attention of the man behind the desk and he picks up a phone, but before contacting the switchboard, he hands the other phone to the SS Oberleutenant to make the call, since it concerns a military matter. He would monitor the conversation with the other phone. After several minutes, the connection to Submarine Headquarters in Lorient is made.

"Hello, this is Kapitanleutnant Godt, staff adjutant to Admiral Dönitz. To whom do I speak?"

Godt's familiar, booming voice reaches Karl's ears and he has difficulty holding back a smile.

"I am SS Oberleutnant Meyer, attached to Gestapo headquarters in Paris. We have a man in custody for questioning as a suspected Resistance fighter or foreign agent. He claims to be a naval officer attached to Lorient."

"What's the man's name, Oberleutnant?"

"His suspected identification and leave papers say he's Kapitanleutnant Karl Heineke."

There's a two-second pause by Godt before he says, "Admiral Dönitz insists on directly handling any inquiries about his submarine commanders. I'll summon him to the phone."

The celebrity status of Admiral Dönitz had reached the SS. "Oh, it won't be necessary to bother the admiral, Kapitanleutnant. Your confirmation will be sufficient," Meyer says.

"No, it won't. Stay on the line while I contact Admiral Dönitz at his New Year's Eve affair, Oberleutnant…and that's an order."

After a pause of three minutes, the admiral speaks in a harsh tone. "This is Admiral Dönitz. What's your problem with Kapitanleutnant Heineke, one of my best U-boat commanders?"

The SS officer's face turns a red blush as he relates the reasons for the arrest.

"You brought him to be interrogated at Gestapo headquarters because he spoke English to his girlfriend and was wearing civilian clothing? Listen to me. If that's Heineke, and I'll confirm that by speaking to him in a moment, you have arrested a hero to the German cause. I have decorated this officer with the Iron Cross. I've sent him out to sea on a U-boat on combat patrols while you SS and Gestapo were enjoying the sights and frills of Paris."

"We didn't know, sir." SS Oberleutenant Meyer's blush has acquired a purple tint from holding his breath and as he stands by the desk, his legs start to shuffle. He turns to the Gestapo agent seated behind the desk, who's listening in. He wants him to take some of the brunt of the admiral's anger. The agent in charge silently waves him off.

"Put Kapitanleutenant Heineke on this phone now," Admiral Dönitz commands.

Karl is handed the phone. "Happy New Year, Admiral. I was interrupted at a brasserie by the Gestapo after I took my first bite of prime meat with a lovely lady by my side. They arrested us both."

"The best of the new year to you, Heineke. I was also interrupted during my dinner. I'll make sure you'll enjoy the rest of the evening and I suppose it will take thirteen days or so before your uniform gets cleaned and repaired. You have my permission to continue in civilian clothing for that period. Your orders may be so noted. Now put me back on with that SS boob."

Karl hands the phone to an extremely nervous Meyer.

"Listen to me, Oberleutenant. This is an order. You will release both the lady and Kapitanleutenant Heineke immediately. You will then return Kapitanleutenant Heineke and his lady friend to the brasserie. You will purchase another meal for them, including the wine of their choice. Any further harassment of them by you or any of the Paris SS will be reported to me. If you do not carry out these orders, I'll make one phone call and have you transferred to the Eastern Front immediately. Is that understood?"

The thought of leaving the tranquility of Paris to fight Russians in the ice and snow makes Meyer's body start to shake. He manages to say, "Yes, sir, Admiral."

"Okay, now...who's in charge of this arrest from the Gestapo end?" Admiral Dönitz asks.

The man behind the desk reluctantly speaks into his phone. "I am Gestapo Station Manager Gerlach, Admiral. We've made a grave mistake and they both will be released immediately."

"If the release is not carried out as I directed, I'll contact Herr Himmler and report this absurdity brought about by his Gestapo in Paris. Is that understood, Herr Gerlach?"

Hearing Himmler's name makes Gerlach's hand holding the phone shake while he says, "Yes, Admiral, sir."

Karl is escorted to the lobby and Marie Paul joins him there. They're whisked away in a staff car to Boulevard Saint-Germain.

They enter Brasserie Albert, where Albert Chabot meets them full of apologies for what he terms an outrage. He hugs both and whispers to Karl. "I was disappointed that I couldn't intercede and prevent your arrest. But for me to interfere would've made the situation worse for you with the possibility that they would close my brasserie."

"I understand Albert." Heineke says.

The SS Oberleutenant confers with Albert and then reaches for his wallet, counting out the amount requested for their meal and wine. Albert summons a waiter and directs him to serve the alcove table a magnum of champagne. Later, the waiter takes the champagne from an ice bucket and removes the cork with a loud pop. While he's pouring the bubbly wine into the two glasses, SS Officer Meyer approaches the table.

He clicks his heals together. "Is everything as ordered, Kapitanleutnant?"

Karl's answer to the affirmative causes Meyer's right arm to come up in a rigid salute, accompanied by the words, "Heil Hitler." Karl doesn't return the salute and Meyer spins around to make a fast exit from the brasserie.

Marie Paul lifts her glass. "To Admiral Dönitz."

The same meal as ordered before their false arrest comes with a special complimentary bottle of Merlot selected by Albert from his wine cellar. As midnight approaches, only a few German uniforms remain at the tables. They have moved their New Year's Eve celebrations out into the nightlife of Paris.

The orchestra is playing slow dance music and Karl holds Marie Paul close as they dance to it. Some of the pieces are French love songs, music that brings back memories of their student years, when Paris was free and the world was at peace. At midnight, 1942 is ushered in with their long kiss while the band plays "Auld Lang Syne."

As they leave for Marie Paul's apartment, both wonder what the war will bring to them in 1942. Karl's vision of being depth-charged emerges and Marie Paul has concerns for her brother and that the German occupation of Paris might turn even more restrictive and cruel.

* * *

For the next thirteen days, the routine for Karl and Marie Paul is that he sleeps late while she's at the Sorbonne lecturing for three hours each morning. Many times when she returns at noon, it's a brunch of an omelet made of fresh eggs and vegetables sent from Marie Paul's parents' farm in Normandy. In the afternoon, they stroll along the Seine or the length of the Avenue Champs Elysees from the Arc de Triumph to the Place de la Concorde, stopping for coffee or a glass of wine at a sidewalk café along the way. They visit the few museums not closed by the war. Marie Paul's favorite is the Rodin.

They make love in the late afternoon and dine later in the Left Bank bistros and brasseries, including Brasserie Albert.

* * *

There time together is fleeting too soon it's time for Marie Paul to see Karl off for Lorient at the Montparnasse train station. They're standing on the train platform. Karl is hesitating to board.

"That's not a tear on your cheek is it, Marie Paul?"

"Oh, Karl, I tried not to cry, but with the uncertainty of this war... when and where will we meet again?"

Karl holds her in his arms until the train starts to move...not ever wanting to let go. He says, "Before it's over I'll come to Paris when ever I can. And when it's over I'll live here with you."

The train starts to move and their kiss is a hurried one before Karl runs to his car and jumps on it throwing his suitcase in front of him

Eastern Sea Frontier

Enemy Action Diary

12 January 1942
1915 hours SS Cyclops *torpedoed off Cape Cod.*

CHAPTER 12

East Bay, January 31, 1942

"Hey, why don't we patrol the same way we did last weekend? One of us stays in the dune, one guy walks the beach for two miles toward P-Town, and the other patrols along the beach beyond Highland Light for the same distance. We'll all keep in touch with those handheld radios Bill gave us."

Iggy says, "Okay, Junie," and Allie nods his approval of the plan.

"If you see or hear anything weird, radio the dune," Junie says. "The guy there will report it to the Coast Guard at Highland Light. So…let's flip to see who stays in the dune, patrols past Highland Light, and goes toward P-Town." Junie tosses a buffalo nickel in the air twice. Each assignment gets made. Junie gets the dune, Allie the beach toward Provincetown, and Iggy is left with Highland Light and beyond.

"I'll keep the charcoal grill burning and the hot chocolate hot so we can warm up when we swap around."

"Okay, Junie. Hey, in a couple of months, my dad is going to take me on a fishing trip to Georges Bank for my birthday…so I can't patrol on that weekend."

"We'll replace you with Betty Fuller. I'd love to get her in the dune all alone."

"What would you do, Junie?" Allie asks. "Read to her from that medical journal?"

Junie scowls an answer. The other two are still laughing when they scramble up the ladder and move off in separate ways down the beach.

* * *

An hour passes before Junie hears Allie's high-pitched voice on his radio. "Geez, you're not gonna believe this, Junie."

"What've you got, Allie?"

"It's a dead body that's washed up on the beach."

"Where are you?"

"I'm about a mile down the beach."

"Okay, stay there. I'll call the Coast Guard at Highland Light and report it."

Soon, Allie sees a Coast Guard jeep approaching him along the surf at high speed. When it reaches him and stops, Bill Childs jumps out of the passenger seat and approaches the body. He notes that the corpse is wearing a life preserver with *SS Cyclops* stenciled on it in black letters. He then radios his adjutant at Highland Light, requesting information on the *Cyclops*.

In a few minutes, the adjutant gets back. "Sir, the *Cyclops* was torpedoed and sunk off Cape Cod on January 12. It was a British cargo steamer of nine thousand and seventy tons, and eighty-seven men were lost from a complement of one hundred eighty-two."

"Okay, thanks, Sweeney. Send an ambulance down the beach about a mile and a half from Highland toward Provincetown to retrieve a body."

Commander Childs then turns toward Allie, who's staring at the bloated corpse as it moves slowly back and forth in the surf. Childs assumes that it's the first time Allie has seen a dead body. His two thoughts intersect. *This man lost his life in the war so near to this shore, and I remain safe away from any such combat. Without having sufficient manpower, I've assigned a fourteen-year-old kid, the son of the woman I love, to patrol a beach and see something as horrible as this.*

Childs approaches Allie, puts a hand on his shoulder, and says, "You did a good job, Allie, finding this sailor and radioing in. We all feel sad about the deaths caused by this war."

CHAPTER 13

Lorient, France
January 31, 1942

"How was Paris, Karl?"

"It was great, Hans. Except for all the German uniforms and vehicles, the city remains the same as I remember it in 1935. My visit with Marie Paul was the best."

"Adjutant Godt told me about your run-in with the Gestapo."

"Yeah, the admiral came through on that with flying colors. How was Augsburg and your family?"

"Augsburg is starting to look like a city preparing for a bombing, Karl. Sand bags all around and anti-aircraft gun emplacements in the city. It's expected that the British and American bombers will go after that diesel engine factory there. The kids and Ingrid are doing fine, but Ingrid will not move them out of the city. We argued about that, but she's stubborn on the issue of leaving Augsburg for the countryside."

They're standing on the deck of U-432, watching the last of the perishable food being lowered below for storage in every available nook and cranny there. There are items like knockwursts and cheeses to be hung from overhead pipes. Potatoes, turnips, radishes, carrots, and canned goods will find a storage space somewhere within the submarine. Fresh water is a priority and as many as fifty-five one-liter tins that will fit into the last available spaces are stored for the long patrol.

The fourteen torpedoes have been loaded in the fore and aft tubes or stored nearby, as well as ammunition for the deck guns.

The diesel fuel tanks are full. During the loading of the last provisions, all crew members not involved in that activity are on the dock out of the way, waiting for the order to board.

When the last of the provisions are in place, the boatswain's mate comes up from below deck and reports that to the captain.

"Okay, Hans, have the rest of the crew board. We sail in an hour."

"I'll so order, Captain, and be ready for all their lack-of-enough-room complaints. I handle that by showing them that I'll be sleeping with two turnips and a knockwurst hanging over my head."

The rest of the crew walks up the gang-plank single-file and boards the U-432, each saluting their captain. Karl returns each salute while taking a cursory look at each man to make sure he's sober and fit for the long patrol.

Two hours later, the U-432 is out of Lorient Harbor, cruising the Atlantic surface on a westerly course. Karl Heineke leaves the bridge and goes below. He retrieves the sealed envelope detailing the Operation Drumbeat orders from a locked drawer in the chart table and makes his way to the captain's nook, dodging provisions hanging from the overhead along the way. He draws the green curtain that separates his nook from the control and radio rooms. He looks at the photo of Marie Paul on his nightstand for a long moment. Karl then heads for the control room to brief the crew on the patrol.

The crew gathers around him. Karl opens the envelope and reads the orders for their part in Operation Drumbeat. "The U-432's patrol along the Eastern coast of the United States will range from the Gulf of Maine to the Cape Cod shores, and extend to the coast off the Carolinas. Ships leaving the ports of Portsmouth, Boston, New York, Norfolk, Charleston, and New Orleans to group in convoys off Halifax heading for England or Russia will be the prime targets. The six other U-boats with which we'll interact are listed on this order. Today we will stay on the surface and set a full-speed course for the East Coast of America, arriving off Cape Cod On February 8. We may extend our patrol to Cape Hatteras if ordered to do so. Do any of you have questions?"

The cook says, "It looks to me like a long patrol, Captain. Will we be getting any provisions along the way?"

"Yes, Gimple, we're scheduled to rendezvous with a *milk cow* submarine on April 6 for food and water provisioning."

* * *

February 9, 1942

The U-*432* is running on the surface eighteen miles off the coast of Massachusetts. It is 11:06 p.m., Eastern Standard time.

Karl Heineke is in the control room perusing a chart showing the coastline of Cape Cod and the nearby islands of Nantucket and Martha's Vineyard.

The radio operator has earphones on and is tuning the frequency dial through the AM band. "Captain, I've tuned into a Boston radio station...it's music, but I don't understand the words." He hands the earphones to Karl.

Karl puts the earphones on and listens. He understands the English lyrics and a pang of sentiment overwhelms him. His thoughts go to when, if ever, he will be with Marie Paul again. He continues to listen to the song:

We'll meet again,
Don't know where,
Don't know when,
But I know we'll meet again some sunny day.

He hands the earphones back to the operator, saying, "Damn this war," in English, which prompts a puzzled look from his radio operator. "Okay, Fritz, no more music and start listening for the sound of propellers. We're in enemy waters."

Hans Topp comes down from his watch on deck.

"See anything interesting up there, Number One?"

"Captain, I'm not sure the Americans know they're at war. I can see the lights from the Boston skyline and those of cars driving along the roads of Cape Cod."

"Don't underestimate them, Hans. They're a sleeping tiger now, but soon they'll wake to carry out their vengeance on us." Using a slang English phrase, Karl says, "So, we should make hay while the sun shines."

Radioman Fritz interrupts them. "Sir, I've picked up some prop noise from a large ship...could be a tanker."

Karl shouts his command: "Clear the deck."

As soon as the deck watch scrambles down though the hatch and it's secure, he gives the order to dive.

Eastern Sea Frontier

Enemy Action Diary

2306 hours February 9, 1942
A Coast Guard plane saw a submarine off Nantucket Light.
Army plane sighted a sub at 34-47N, 75-00W.

CHAPTER 14

East Bay, February 9, 1942

"Should I confront him about his affair with Lois Cohen, Bill?"

Bill Childs is silent for what seems like too long to her before giving an answer to Barbara Sheffield's question.

It's early on Monday morning and they're sitting in Barbara's car at a secluded beach front on the bay side of Cape Cod, watching the sun rise.

"If you're sure about it, you have to do so. But during that same confrontation, shouldn't you tell him about us?"

Barbara's eyes leave his troubled expression and look out on the bay for a long moment before she answers. "It's the kids. It's more about them than him. It's Allie and Junie Cohen that I don't want to hurt. Danny and Jane are away from all this for now."

"How close is Doctor Sheffield to Allie, Barbara?"

She thinks about that for a moment before she answers. "It's sort of an arm's length relationship. He's as cold toward Allie as he is to me and was very upset when I became pregnant with him."

"How does Allie feel about his dad?"

"Oh, I guess he respects him, but lately the connection between you and Allie is a much closer one. He adores you."

"By the way, I felt bad about Allie having to come across that body that washed up from the *Cyclops*. There could be more of them. Do you want him to continue patrolling the beach?"

"He wouldn't have it any other way, Bill. They all grow up fast in times of war and if this goes on much longer, his dune buddies and he could be in the midst of things much worse than that."

"Good. I need him because we're still short-handed for beach patrols."

The sun was peaking over the Boston skyline far across the bay when Bill checked his wristwatch. "I've got to get back to Highland Light; the U-boat activity off the coast is increasing. Where are we with approaching your husband about us and the Cohen lady?"

"Oh, shit, Bill. This is not going to be easy. On the other hand, this is a small town and I'm sure tongues are wagging already."

Bill takes her in his arms. When the kiss finishes, he puts both his palms on her cheeks and looks into her eyes. "Why don't you do this in two pieces? You confront him about his affair, going on right in your house, and save any confessions about us for another time when that settles in. I think this will protect Allie and Junie from getting it all at once. What do you think about doing it that way?"

Again, Barbara looks out on the bay waters where the sun, now above the horizon, has painted the ripples a burnt orange color. "I'll get that done this morning before Lois arrives for work."

They leave Barbara's car and walk to Bill's jeep, where they lock in an embrace before both drive off in separate vehicles toward their separate tasks.

* * *

Barbara arrives home at 8 a.m., parks her car, and meets Allie in the driveway as he heads for school.

"Hey, Mom, I missed you. Were you checking out the sunrise on the bay side as usual? Anyway, Dad and I had breakfast."

Barbara gives her son a hug then asks, "What did you have for breakfast?"

"He cooked cereal and smothered it on top with molasses… Yuck!"

She smiles and gives Allie another hug and kiss on the cheek before asking him, "Where's your dad now?"

"He's in his office."

Allie skips off down the driveway and his mom enters the house and goes directly to her husband's office.

It's rare for her to enter his sanctuary, but she opens the door without knocking.

The doctor looks up from his desk abruptly as if surprised to see her. "Hello, Barbara, what's up?"

"We need to talk."

"Okay, just give me a couple of minutes to finish looking at the charts of my first patients today."

Barbara places her hands on her hips and glares at him. "It's important."

He stares her down. "I said in a few minutes."

She turns and stomps off to a chair in the waiting room, thinking, *I'm always last among his priorities. The bastard!*

Five minutes go by and she's about to go back to his office when the fire chief, John Davis, bursts into the waiting room, out of breath.

"Mrs. Sheffield, is the doctor in his office?"

"Yes, he's sitting at his desk."

"I need him. We have an emergency. In about an hour, survivors from a torpedoed tanker off Nantucket will be brought to the East Bay town wharf for evacuation to the Boston hospitals by ambulance. There'll be some with burns and other injuries requiring first aid before they're evacuated."

The loud words from the fire chief penetrate Doctor Sheffield's inner sanctum. He comes through the door with his coat on, carrying two leather satchels filled with medical supplies.

"Okay, John, I'm headed for the town wharf. Get to the Red Cross and make sure they bring a good supply of blankets and bandages."

They both leave the office in a rush. Over his shoulder on the way out, the doctor says, "Barbara, you can use your nurse's training today." A sneer curls his lips when he says that before he stops at the threshold and adds, "Oh, and tell Lois when she comes in where I am and that I need her at the town wharf."

Barbara leaves the office and goes to her room. She changes into slacks and a flannel shirt, and puts on a sweater and leather jacket. While she's hurrying to her car, Lois walks up the driveway. As Barbara opens her car door, she yells out, "He's at the town wharf and needs you."

Barbara gets into the car and slams the door while Lois stands in the driveway mouthing questions Barbara can't hear…and in any case would be loath to answer.

* * *

The scene at the town wharf is calm while all are preparing for the survivors to land. The day is raw and bleak, as days are when East Bay is more sea than land.

It was early morning, shortly before seven, when the call came from the Coast Guard to the fire chief, John Davis, acting as civil defense chairman, to stand by for survivors coming ashore. In short order he mustered ambulances and nurses, doctors from surrounding towns, auxiliary police, and Red Cross volunteers. Other East Bay volunteers, including Elizabeth Ann Broderick and Gina Posada, were brewing soup and coffee in the Land's End Hotel kitchen. The now empty hotel near the town wharf will be the initial survivor treatment center before the evacuation to Boston hospitals takes place. Dr. Sheffield is put in charge of the medical entity in the hotel ballroom, now lined with cots.

The houses and schools of East Bay empty as all townspeople head down to the wharf. They wait silently behind barriers set by the police. Finally, a Coast Guard cutter, followed by two of East Bay's fishing boats, appears through the harbor fog. One of the trawlers is the *Elizabeth Ann*, owned by Captain Pete Broderick. His son Iggy, standing with his friends Junie and Allie, is the first to see it. He yells out, "It's my dad's boat…he's got survivors!"

The three boats dock and the ambulances move in close. The most seriously injured survivors are taken by stretcher to the ambulances for the short ride to the hotel. Those that can walk are wrapped in blankets by the volunteers and helped to the hotel dining room, where they are given hot soup, coffee, cigarettes, and food, if asked for. Some of the crew has been immersed in the cold Atlantic for an hour before being hauled into their lifeboats and away from a blazing sea fueled by gasoline. Then they waited for the rescue ships that arrived four hours after they were torpedoed, around midnight. Some of the men are suffering from hyperthermia.

Dr. Sheffield uses his recently acquired burn procedure expertise to treat the victims of that horror. They are bathed in a saline solution to prevent infection, swathed in bandages, and given a shot of morphine then are transferred to the waiting ambulances for the two-hour trip to Boston. Nurse Lois Cohen is by the doctor's side, assisting him with the treatment.

Barbara Sheffield is in the hotel dinning room, caring for the walking wounded. She cleans their cuts, applies splints and bandages, and supplies aspirin while trying to cheer them up. She performs with professional ease, and the men address her as *nurse*…a title she doesn't deny.

Bill Childs arrives with six Coast Guard medics and she puts them to work. Those survivors with minor injuries that can walk are loaded on buses to be evacuated to the clinic at Camp Edwards on the Cape.

When the dining room is empty of tanker crewmembers, Barbara takes the opportunity to approach Bill, who's just leaving. She beckons him toward the coat closet and when he enters, she closes the door. They embrace and after a long, full, body-molded kiss, they part.

"Quite a morning, Bill, isn't it?"

"Yeah. Were you able to talk with your husband?"

"No, that was interrupted by the survivor landing."

"Just as well. Maybe it's best to let it ride for awhile. After seeing those poor bastards come in from that torpedoed tanker, I've made a decision to request sea duty aboard a destroyer. I can't stand being on shore and not doing anything about those German U-boats blasting our unarmed ships."

"What does that mean?" Her eyes moisten. "Will you be leaving East Bay?"

"I'll be out of some port on the East Coast if my request goes through. I was an executive officer onboard a Navy destroyer before, so there won't be much training required. It will mean going back to the Navy, but that shouldn't be a problem. Hopefully, I'll get to captain a destroyer."

"Wow…in war, things happen fast." Barbara takes in a deep breath and expels it, finishing her thought: *Happiness rushed at me as fast as it's running away. I guess all wartime romance is rushed.*

"I won't be far from you. If it's Boston, you can meet me there when my ship comes into port."

"I understand how you feel about getting into the action, Bill. Please be careful. You are my first love. Let's have another sunrise on the bay side soon, okay?"

"I'll be at our place at seven on Saturday. I need a couple of days to push through my transfer to Navy sea duty." He takes her in his arms and holds her close while they kiss.

They both leave the cloakroom together just as Gina Posada and Elizabeth Ann Broderick enter the dining room after they've finished washing dishes in the hotel kitchen. They pass by and Gina says, "Hello Barbara, Commander Childs."

Barbara nods her head; her cheeks are flush.

When Gina and Elizabeth Ann reach the parking lot, Gina says, "Looks like we have another East Bay love affair, Betty. It could be one that's too hot to cool down."

CHAPTER 15

On Board U-432
February 10, 1942

"That tanker we torpedoed early this morning off Nantucket Island was nine thousand six hundred tons, Captain." Hans Topp is reading that information from a Lloyd's of London ship registry.

"Yes, Hans, the way it exploded after the second torpedo hit tells me it was loaded with aircraft gasoline." Karl Heineke shakes his head. "I wanted to get away from there as fast as possible. We can't pick up survivors, by the admiral's order, and I knew there'd be some in the water. Poor devils… It's a cruel war, Hans, and I wish it would end soon so I could feel human again."

Hans was about to comment when they were interrupted by Fritz, the radio operator. "I just recorded an *Enigma* message from the admiral."

"Read it, Fritz," Karl says.

"'Kapitanleutenant Heineke, the U-432 will proceed to Cape Hatteras for patrol. It's a happy hunting ground. Good hunting, Admiral Dönitz.'"

Karl bends over the chart table and studies the chart. "It looks like we can be off Cape Hatteras tomorrow evening if we run on the surface, Hans. We can patrol in those waters before our rendezvous with the milk cow boat on April 6 at Georges Bank, when that re-provisioning is scheduled. Then we'll patrol Cape Cod until we return to Lorient."

"Yeah, we'll be needing food, water, and torpedoes by then, Karl."

91

CHAPTER 16

East Bay, February 14, 1942

On this Saturday morning, the sunrise is a spectacular one as a myriad of colors paints the sky and ocean surrounding Cape Cod Bay. Barbara Sheffield and Bill Childs are viewing this splendor through the windshield of her car.

"Well, my transfer to sea duty and back to the Navy has been approved."

"That was fast, Bill."

"Seems like the U-boat activity off the coast and my past experience on a cutter helped move it along through channels."

"Any details on where you'll be sent?"

Bill turns away from the sunrise and looks at Barbara with an expression of concern. "It's not going to be good for us. Because of the U-boat activity off the coast of the Carolinas, I'm going to be assigned to a new destroyer that'll be operating out of Charleston, South Carolina. After some sea trials, I may be given command of that ship."

Barbara is silent for a few seconds while she sorts out her feelings before she says, "I'm happy for you. I know it's what you want. Perhaps it's fate that the war that brought you here is now taking you away from me."

"It's not the end for us. I don't want it to be, Barbara. I'll keep close touch and we'll soon be together again. Maybe a visit by you... Charleston is a great city."

"When do you leave? Allie will be disappointed."

"Monday, and I plan on stopping by the dune today to say goodbye to him and the boys."

Her expression is one of resolve. She hugs his neck, kisses him, and says, "I'll miss you, but I'll be busy. I've enrolled in an accelerated registered nurse program at Cape Cod Hospital. The course will make me an RN in eighteen months. They need nurses because so many have gone to war."

"Hey, the best thing to come out of this is that we're both doing the things we want to. The worst part is doing them without each other around." He turns to meet her kiss and as it becomes more intense, he reaches for the buttons on her blouse.

"Oh, Bill, not here."

When the last one is unbuttoned, he says, "Yes, here."

The Dune

The dune is winterized. That large canvas tent previously used to cover the boys' possessions now stretches over four two-by-fours and is anchored by sand piled on its edges to form a waterproof roof. The light and heat are supplied by two Coleman lanterns vented by the opening for the ladder. Two cots have been supplied by the Coast Guard and the bedding consists of sleeping bags.

It's early on Saturday morning and the boys' beach patrol is about to commence. They're sitting on the cots, sipping hot chocolate heated by a Sterno can and laughing about their overexuberance during the scrap metal and rubber drive on Friday.

"Junie, are you going to give Alice Trimble back her bike before it's melted down to be part of a Sherman tank?"

"I have to...her mother called mine, even though it's a piece of junk."

"I snatched a tire out of old Charlie Davis's yard," Allie says. "He wasn't too happy and claimed it was his spare."

"All for the war effort, guys." Junie then changes the subject to their activity today. "Because of that torpedoed tanker off Nantucket, your beach patrol this morning might turn up some weird stuff." He looks at Iggy and then his eyes linger awhile on Allie with concern.

"You mean like another body might wash up?"

"It's possible, Allie. Why don't the two of you do the patrol together? You can radio me if anything shows up."

They both climb the ladder and start down the beach toward Highland Light. It's not long before they see that the tide has brought in an oily, rainbow-like covering that smells of gasoline. When they turn down the beach toward Provincetown, they find more debris awash. There are life jackets, wooden pallets, and an empty lifeboat, but to Allie's relief, there are no dead bodies awash in the surf. When they radio their find to Junie at the dune, he has some news.

"Commander Childs just radioed that he's on his way and he wants to meet you guys at the dune."

A short time later, they're back inside the dune, waiting for Bill. As they drink more of the Sterno-heated hot chocolate, they hear the Coast Guard jeep pull up outside.

Bill peeks down through the ladder opening and says, "Wow, this outpost has really been improved. Do I have your permission to come aboard?"

They stand, smile, and utter a chorus of, "Sure," "of course," and "yes, sir."

Childs comes down the ladder and sits down on a cot next to Allie. "I have some news...I'm leaving for sea duty on Monday."

The shock shows on all three of their faces. Allie breaks their silence with, "So soon? I thought you'd be here all through the war."

"I put in for the transfer. The war is too near to us now and I want to fight it offshore."

"Are you gonna get those U-boats before they torpedo more ships like the one off Nantucket?"

"That's the idea, Junie."

"Will anything change with us?" Allie asks.

"No, the Coast Guard still needs you guys."

"Who'll take your place?"

"My replacement is sitting in the jeep, waiting to meet you boys, Junie. His name is Lieutenant Commander Scott Lee."

They all scramble up the ladder and walk to the jeep. A tall, rugged redhead leaves the passenger seat and saunters over toward them, shaking each of the boy's hands. His grin spreads his chubby cheeks from ear to ear.

"I've heard all about what a good job of patrolling this beach y'all have been doing." His deep Southern accent gives a hint of his home region before he says, "I'm from Georgia. Y'all keep doing what you were doing for Commander Childs, and we'll get along just fine. Oh, and I may need you for some Friday night beach patrolling...that okay?"

Junie looks at each of his friends as they nod their heads before he answers for them. "Yes, sir, we can do that."

"Good...and y'all call me Scott. I'm just an ol' rambling wreck football lineman from Georgia Tech who went Coast Guard."

The boys say goodbye to Bill with handshakes. Bill hesitates a few seconds before he hugs Allie. Close to his ear, he says, "I'm going to miss you."

That whisper brings a tear to one of Allie's eyes that he hopes will go unnoticed by his friends.

* * *

As the jeep moves beside the surf toward Highland Light, Bill tells Scott, "Those kids are very special to me. I'd like you to watch over them, Scott."

"Yes, sir. I'll be their big ol' mother hen."

"Oh, and on those Friday night beach patrols for them, make sure blackout rules apply. A recent intelligence alert tells about the Germans planning to land saboteurs on our shores by submarine."

"I'll do that. Man, I'd sure like to sack a few of those Nazi bastards."

Eastern Sea Frontier

Enemy Action Diary

March 14, 1942
0245 hrs. Report from a fisherman, long submarine with masthead and side navigation lights burning passed within 100 yards going in southerly direction. Second submarine was about one-half mile behind and showed no lights. It was observed with binoculars. Position of fisherman 22 miles NW by W from Nantucket light.

* * *

March 29, 1942
1430 hours. Coast Guard reports intercept {message} from SS City Of New York: *"74-34 W. Going down."*

CHAPTER 17

East Bay, April 5, 1942

"Pete, are you sure it'll be safe to fish the Georges Bank? All those German subs around…and taking our son with you. I don't like it one bit."

Pete and Elizabeth Ann Broderick are having their customary Friday evening cocktail before dinner. They're waiting for Gina and Antonio Posada to arrive and join them in a birthday dinner for Iggy.

Pete sets his short glass half-filled with bourbon over ice on the kitchen table and says, "My trawler is small potatoes for the U-boats. They're after large tankers and cargo ships…and according to the Coast Guard, most of the action is now off Cape Hatteras."

"I suppose it'll be alright. If Ignatius doesn't go with you as promised for his birthday, he'll be disappointed. How long will you be out?"

"I'll leave the harbor at 4 a.m. tomorrow morning and be back Monday evening. Iggy will only miss one day of school."

Antonio arrives with Gina. He's carrying a pail of clams for steaming and two quart bottles of Narragansett beer. Gina has a gift for Iggy wrapped in silver paper with a blue bow. It's a hand-made fisherman's sweater she knitted with cable stitching.

Pete finishes the last of his bourbon and opens one of the Narragansett bottles. The men sip the beer while waiting for the steamers to be served from the kitchen.

Elizabeth Ann washes the sand from the clams. She puts three dozen in a pot, adds an inch of water and a handful of chopped celery, and places the pot on top of the wood stove. Then she prepares the main meal, consisting of potatoes for mashing, carrots, and canned peas to accompany the pork roast, with a fresh clam chowder as a starter. Iggy's birthday cake was made earlier and it now sits on a kitchen counter graced with fourteen candles. The ladies catch up on East Bay gossip while sipping sherry and tending to the meal.

"Well, that love affair has been interrupted."

"Which one...is it Lois and the doctor or Barbara and that Coast Guard officer, Gina?

"Oh, haven't you heard the latest?" Gina takes a sip of her sherry and says, "Well, Bill Childs requested sea duty and got it. He left for Charleston, South Carolina, on Monday."

"So, do you think that's the end for them?"

"Maybe, Betty, but guess who's going to nurse's training in Hyannis with some of it taking place in Boston?"

"Barbara? Good, she really wanted that and deserves it. I'm happy for her. Though it's kind of sad that she'll be so far away from the love she's finally found."

Gina takes another sip of her sherry, squints her eyes, and says, "Maybe, but I hear the trains are still running between Boston and Charleston, South Carolina."

Elizabeth Ann smiles at Gina's innuendo and then changes the subject to her son. "Larry finished Marine Corps boot camp and has been sent to San Diego for combat training."

"I got a letter from Marcello yesterday. He's practicing amphibian landings in Texas." Gina's eyes close when she says, "I don't like this. I think our Army will be sent to Africa to help the English fight the Germans there."

"Did you get that small banner with the blue star on it to hang in your window, Gina? It's to show that you've got a son or daughter serving in the military. Somehow, I don't want one yet."

"I have one. Maybe you don't want that banner because of the one Ellie Cole has. It has a gold star because her son was killed at Pearl Harbor." A sob came from Gina as she said that.

"Jesus, Mary, and Joseph, Gina...can we get back to the town gossip?"

In the other room, Iggy joins the men at the table as the steamed clams are served. They shuck them and dip each into a cup of broth then into one of melted butter.

"Happy birthday, Iggy. You ready to go fishing?"

"I can't wait to go, Mr. Posada."

"Good, the *Elizabeth Ann* is all fueled and ice is in the hole".

* * *

At a little after 4 a.m. the next morning, the *Elizabeth Ann* leaves East Bay Harbor for the Georges Bank. After helping with the un-docking, Iggy snuggles down in the bow, looking out to sea as they clear the harbor and pass by Highland Light.

CHAPTER 18

On Board the U-432, Georges Bank
April 6, 1942

"Have you sighted our milk cow, Hans? It's now seven hours late. I've rechecked our rendezvous point and we're where we should be. Fritz has been trying to raise them on the radio without any luck."

Karl Heineke is bent over the chart table, talking on the interphone to Hans Topp, who's on deck searching the horizon for any sign of the supply ship.

"No, Captain, nothing in sight."

"Okay, come below and leave two men on deck to keep the watch."

When Hans arrives in the control room, he looks at his captain with a worried expression. "We have one torpedo left and enough food and water for only three days, even with rationing. The humidity off the Carolinas caused many of the perishables to rot. That last ship we torpedoed was the *SS City of New York*, according to the Lloyd's register, the tonnage was over 9000 and it's all about tonnage because it's the way our Fuehrer keeps score."

"Great, after sinking six ships off Hatteras and two off Cape Cod for a successful patrol, the damn milk cow doesn't show up." Karl looks over at Fritz. "Any luck in contacting them?"

The radioman holds up his hand, indicating that a message is coming through on *Enigma* from Lorient. A few minutes go by before he says, "Bad news, Captain. The milk cow was attacked by an aircraft and sunk eighty miles east of our rendezvous position."

"Shit, it's a nine-day sail to Lorient and we have three days of food and water with just enough fuel to make it there." Heineke takes a deep breath before he orders, "Clear the deck. We're going to submerge and look around Georges Bank for a replacement to our lost milk cow. There should be some American or Canadian fishing boats out here."

* * *

Heineke scans Georges Bank for two hours and finally spots a trawler. Through the optics of his periscope, he watches the fishing boat for a while until he orders the helmsman to maneuver closer so he can read the name of the boat. He sees that the crew of the *Elizabeth Ann*, out of East Bay, consists of two men and a young boy, and they're dumping their catch into the hole. "Hans, I think we've found our milk cow replacement. Take a look."

Hans looks through the periscope as the U-boat moves in alongside the trawler. "There's plenty of fish there for the taking, Karl."

"Yes, but I'd rather not let our piracy act rough anyone up in their crew. Let's surface beside them. Have both deck guns manned and prepare a rubber raft for boarding. I'll talk to the trawler captain through a megaphone."

CHAPTER 19

"Okay, Antonio, after this trawl, we'll head for home."

Pete Broderick looks out where screaming gulls are anticipating some fallout from a net loaded with hake, haddock, and codfish as it's winched on board. "This catch should fill the hole."

"Great trip, Captain. Iggy must've brought us his birthday luck."

Iggy scrambles aft from his favorite place on the bow and starts to help off-load the catch. After the net is empty, the trawler's hole is filled to the deck boards and a layer of ice is shoveled in to cover the wiggling fish there.

When he finishes helping to empty the net of the last catch, Iggy returns to his watch at the bow. A squawking seagull draws his attention from straight ahead to the ocean surface on the starboard side of the boat. When he sees a periscope cutting a small wake beside the *Elizabeth Ann*, Iggy shouts out to his dad.

Pete Broderick spots the periscope and reaches for his radio microphone. He calls in the *Elizabeth Ann*'s position and the sub sighting on that special frequency allocated by the First Naval District.

Iggy's eyes pop open in disbelief when, alongside the trawler's starboard side, a U-boat surfaces. As the sea water drains off its sleek black hull, several men climb from the conning tower onto the deck of the submarine.

Antonio Posada comes out of the wheelhouse. "Iggy, it's a German U-boat. Let's be careful."

Iggy's fear is tinged with curiosity. "Gee, it's huge, Mr. Posada. What do they want with us?"

Before Antonio can attempt an answer to Iggy's question, they see a man with a white hat raise a megaphone to his mouth.

"Ahoy, captain of the *Elizabeth Ann*." The voice comes to them loud and in clear English.

Pete leaves the wheelhouse and goes to the rail on the starboard side. He cups both hands beside his mouth and yells, "I'm Captain Peter Broderick. What do you want?"

"Captain Broderick, I am Kapitanleutnant Heineke of the German Navy, commander of this U-boat. We are very low on food and water. I would like some fish and all the water you can spare. May I have your permission to come on board your boat?"

Pete Broderick looks over at the two large guns on the U-boat. They are manned by sailors and pointed at the *Elizabeth Ann*. Pete yells his answer, "I'm not sure I have any choice, Captain."

Two of the U-boat crewmembers, along with their captain, climb into a rubber raft and shove off toward the *Elizabeth Ann*. When they board the trawler, Pete notices they're not armed.

Heineke approaches Broderick and offers a handshake with a smile. Pete is reluctant at first, but accepts Heineke's hand without returning the smile. He waits for this German who speaks perfect English to voice his request.

"I wouldn't be doing this, Captain, but my crew will starve if I don't. I have American dollars to pay for the fish and water, but I suggest that you refuse that payment and consider this an act of piracy. As you know, accepting payment would be aiding and abetting your enemy and could be considered treason."

Pete Broderick points to the U-boat. "I have no choice with those deck guns trained on me, so let's get this over with." His thought is, *I want this finished and to be underway before an aircraft or destroyer converges on the position I radioed to the First Naval District. I don't want the* Elizabeth Ann *in the midst of that battle.*

"Very well. I'd like you to remain where you are and not to go near your radio. I've decided not to disable it as a courtesy, and I'll be out of here before you can alert destroyers or aircraft as to my position."

The two U-boat crewmembers had returned to U-432 and come back to the *Elizabeth Ann* with four empty wooden boxes. The deck hatch to the hole is opened and the men start to load the fish into the boxes. When they finish, they put the fish in the raft and row over to the U-boat to off-load it.

Heineke estimates that each box contains about twenty-five pounds of fish for a total of around one hundred pounds. The fish added to the remaining cans of evaporated milk and potatoes will provide enough fish chowder servings to feed his forty-three-man crew during the nine-day trip to Lorient. "Captain, how much water can you spare?"

"I have only one twenty-gallon container left besides what I need for my trip home. But I've got three bags of ice left over. You can use the ice to keep the fish fresh and when it melts, catch it for drinking water."

"Thank you for you kindness, Captain Broderick."

Heineke's men load the water and ice into the raft and take it to the U-boat. While Heineke waits for them to return for him, he approaches Iggy, who's watching the drama unfold at the rail with nervous apprehension.

"Hello. Are you the son of the captain?"

Before Iggy answers, he glances at his dad for the okay. When Pete Broderick nods his head, he says, "Yes, sir, I'm Ignatius...but mostly everyone calls me Iggy, except my mom."

"How old are you, Iggy?"

"I just turned fourteen today."

"Happy birthday. I hope we didn't scare you too much. Anyway, we'll be gone soon and you'll be on your way home." He then reaches in his jacket and hands Iggy a fountain pen with the insignia of the German Submarine Service inscribed on it. "Here's a little souvenir to show your friends."

As Heineke climbs into the raft and leaves the trawler to return to U-432, he salutes Pete and says, "Thank you, Captain Broderick. Sorry, but this was necessary because my supply ship was sunk. Please stay away from the radio until we're out of sight. We'll be on the surface with deck guns trained on you."

Soon, the U-432 starts to rapidly sail east and when it is out of sight, Pete moves from the rail to the wheelhouse and radios the First Naval District with an update on U-432's course. That information is relayed to a B-25 bomber airborne on an Atlantic patrol out of Westover Air Base in Massachusetts. It's already on a heading toward the U-boat, based on Pete's earlier clandestine radio report to the First Naval District in Boston.

Soon, the B-25 passes over the *Elizabeth Ann* and wiggles its wings while flying two- hundred feet above the waves at two hundred and eighty-five miles per hour on its chase toward the eastern horizon.

CHAPTER 20

"Hans, add another lookout on deck to the two men already there. The captain of that trawler is sure to have gotten on the radio about us."

"Maybe we should have smashed his radio, Karl."

"I didn't want to do that. That trawler captain seemed like a good guy and...the kid."

"Weisel, go up on deck watch with the other two. Okay, the additional watch is on deck, sir."

"Good, we'll continue at full speed. I want to get off Georges Bank and into deeper water in case of visitors. Is the fish chowder being prepared by the cook, Hans?"

"Yes, the first of many more chowders to come is simmering in the galley."

Heineke's chuckle stops when the report from the deck comes over the interphone at scream level: "An aircraft is approaching fast from the west at a low level."

"We're on our way below." The command from Heineke to the helmsman is one of caution. "Start a shallow dive. I want to get those three men below before we dive deep."

As he says this, two pairs of legs belonging to the lookouts come through the hatch. Before the third could make it, the sound of machine gun fire is heard, followed by the thud of two bombs exploding on each side of the hull.

Heineke scrambles up through the conning tower and down to a deck already awash with half a meter of sea water. The third man is kneeling down, hanging onto the ladder with his left arm. The shirt on his right arm is torn and soaked with blood. He appears to be in shock.

"Okay, Weisel, we don't have much time before that plane makes another pass." Heineke gets behind him and pushes Weisel up the ladder, where Hans and another man guide the injured sailor down through the hatch and below. Heineke follows him down and shouts a command.

"Helmsman, deep dive, and all crew rush forward...now!"

The plane starts another pass before the boat can fully submerge. Multiple machine gun bullets *rat-a-tat-tat* against the hull of U-432. The crew feels the concussion of several bombs with fuses set to detonate below the U-boat.

"He's got a couple more passes before he's done." Heineke looks over at the incline meter. "Okay, Helmsman, level off at a depth of thirty meters. Can you get a reading on how far it is to the bottom?"

"Yes, sir, we're only fifteen meters from there."

"Alright, we need more depth than that. Stay on a heading of due east until we get off Georges Bank and into deeper water. Most likely his bombs are fused to detonate in shallower water, like they were on his first pass." Heineke looks over at Hans, who's administering first aid to Weisel with another crewmember. "How's he doing, Hans?"

"We've stopped the blood with a tourniquet and given him morphine but there's a piece of shrapnel lodged in the muscle of his right arm."

U-432 is jolted by the bombs dropped by the B-25's third pass. One of them explodes on deck near the conning tower.

"Engineer, give me a damage report," Heineke says while holding on to the chart table as the sub rocks in response to the concussion of that direct hit.

The engineer reports: "Sir, there's some leaking but there's no serious internal damage. I'll evaluate the damage on deck when we surface."

"What depth do you have to the bottom, Helmsman?"

"Looks like we're coming off the continental shelf and approaching deeper water, Captain."

"Good. Take us down to sixty meters."

Heineke waits for next pass by the B-25. He takes a deep breath as its bombs explode a non-lethal distance above the U-432 before saying, "His bombs' fuses are set to explode at our crash dive depth...not deep."

After one more pass by the B-25, the shock felt by the explosions cease. Then the captain tells Hans, "We'll run on course, silent and deep, for one hour before surfacing to assess any external damage caused by that direct hit on deck. Hans, see to it that the cook serves everyone a bowl of fish chowder and a ration of water. I'll have a look at Weisel's arm."

He turns to the young man. "How do you feel, sailor?"

"I'm in pain every time I move my arm, sir. But it could've been worse if you didn't get me below before that plane's next pass."

Heineke inspects Weisel's arm and sees a jagged piece of shrapnel protruding out of his muscle there. "We're going to remove that. It's what's giving you the pain." He shouts over to Hans, who's at the chart table finishing his chowder. "Do you have something strong for Weisel to ease his pain and sterilize his wound?"

Hans's expression shows surprise that the captain might know of his hidden bottle. "Yes, sir, I have a bottle of French Calvados. I'll get it."

Hans returns with the bottle and Heineke pours a coffee mug half full of the brown liquor, handing it to Weisel. "Drink this in three gulps two minutes apart. Then we'll splash some on your wound to sterilize it."

While waiting, he pours himself and Hans a smaller amount and they down it in one gulp. After Heineke drinks his, he grimaces and says, "No bacteria could live after being splashed with this stuff, Hans."

Hans grins. "It's the very best, sir."

Heineke selects a pair of needle-nose pliers from the engineer's tool box and then splashes some of the Calvados on his hands, the pliers, and Weisel's wound. He attaches the pliers to the piece of shrapnel. With one deft stroke Heineke extracts the shiny two-inch shard of metal as Weisel winces and expels a breath held for ten seconds. The wound is then cleaned and bandaged.

Heineke wraps the shrapnel in a piece of bandage and hands it to Weisel. "Here's a souvenir for your kids and grandchildren."

* * *

After an hour, the U-432 surfaces and continues underway while the damage on deck is assessed.

The engineer reports: "Captain, there's twisted metal on the deck where the bomb hit, but it didn't penetrate the pressure hull. The hull could be cracked, but that will have to be determined in port. The machine gun bullets have pockmarked the deck and hull, both deck rails have been blown overboard, and a deck gun damaged. I'll make the preliminary repairs, but the final work must be done in Lorient."

As the U-432 heads on a course toward Lorient, Heineke retires to the captain's nook. The cook comes by with a plate containing a whole fried haddock and a potato, and serves it with a mug of black coffee.

"Thanks, Gimple. Please make sure Weisel gets a whole piece of fish with his chowder. He needs that protein it to help the healing."

As the cook pulls the green curtain to close the captain's nook, he says, "Yes, sir, I'll feed him well."

After eating, Heineke strips down to shorts and a sweater and lies down on his bunk. He looks over at the photo of Marie Paul and says out loud, "First time I've been attacked by an American airplane. Their submarine defense is getting better. Could be the addition of that radio direction and range device that intelligence says the Americans have in their planes. They see us before we see them. I'll contact you from Lorient, Marie Paul…if this U-boat has enough diesel fuel to reach France."

Soon Heineke drifts into a deep sleep—a few hours of reprieve from the horrors of war.

Eastern Sea Frontier Bulletin, April 1942

From the beginning of the war, there has been a belief that enemy agents or sympathizers have been assisting U-boats in their campaigns. Such assistance could have many forms: fueling the submarines from isolated places along the coast, radioing information about ship departures, meeting them at sea in small boats filled with oil and provisions.

There have also been rumors about neutral vessels or German supply ships that lie off the coast to tend the submarines. Thus far, it has been difficult if not impossible to obtain confirmation of these reasonable beliefs.

CHAPTER 21

East Bay, April 6, 1942

"Dad, there's a Coast Guard boat cutting in front of us."

They entered East Bay Harbor just as the sun was setting on Monday evening.

"Yeah, I see it…probably it's a reception committee because of the German U-boat."

"We didn't do anything wrong, did we?"

"No, son, but we may have to convince the Navy and Coast Guard of that."

As they approach their mooring place, Iggy sees several men in blue overcoats and white hats standing on the dock. Antonio and Iggy jump on the dock to tie up the *Elizabeth Ann*. When they finish, an officer wearing more gold braid on his hat and coat than the others steps forward to hail Pete Broderick.

"Captain Broderick, I'm Navy Captain Johnson of First Naval. We're here to debrief you on the incident involving the enemy U-boat. May I come aboard?"

"Sure…only my mate and son will be unloading the fish while we talk."

"I'd rather have all of you in on this, Captain."

"Okay, let's get it over with so we can get the fish to the buyer."

Captain Johnson comes on board the trawler, along with five other uniformed men. He joins Pete in the wheelhouse and is followed there by a Lieutenant Commander carrying a clipboard. The others start looking around the boat.

"Please understand, Captain, we consider this a serious incident subject to an investigation."

"I understand, but here's the whole story. I was boarded by a German submarine." Pete points at the chart table. "Right here and I reported my position to First Naval before the sub surfaced and after it left. It was an act of piracy on their part. They wanted fish and water and I gave both to them because the guns of their U-boat were trained on us."

The Lieutenant Commander is writing down Pete's words on the clipboard as he speaks. He pauses when Captain Johnson asks a question.

"Did the Germans pay you for the water and fish?"

"No. As I said, I was forced to give it up."

"Did they give anything else as compensation?"

Iggy is fondling the pen in his jacket pocket given to him by Heineke when he says, "Dad, how about the pen?"

"The U-boat captain gave my son a fountain pen as a souvenir."

Captain Johnson calls out to an officer on the deck of the *Elizabeth Ann*. "Grogan, we may have something for you."

The officer enters the wheelhouse and is introduced as Commander Grogan of the Office of Special Investigation (OSI).

"Grogan, the boy was given a pen by the U-boat captain."

Grogan says, "I must confiscate it. There's no telling what tricks the Germans are up to."

Iggy looks over at his father and after Pete nods an approval, he reaches in his jacket pocket and hands the pen to Grogan, who accepts it by having Iggy drop it into an envelope that he places into a leather briefcase.

"We'll run some tests on this pen and return it if nothing shows up."

"Okay, Grogan, is there anything else?"

"Well, Captain Johnson, we've searched the boat thoroughly for any hidden cash. I'll have two of my men stand by while the fish are unloaded to make sure there's nothing concealed there. I'd like to do a body search on the crew for any large amounts of cash."

Captain Johnson detects that the irritation on Broderick's face is about to explode as indignant rage. "Captain, we've had reports of fishing boats who've supplied provisions to German U-boats and we must clear you of that crime."

After their pockets are searched, Johnson reaches for Broderick's hand and shakes it. "Thank you for that fast initial alert and the updated position of that U-boat afterwards. We were able to dispatch a B-25 sub-chasing aircraft as a result and our plane attacked that sub. We're not sure if it was sunk, but we know it has been damaged. I'll get back to Boston now, make out my incident report, and get a copy to you for a signature in a few days."

All but two of the Navy men leave the trawler and depart in one of the staff cars parked near the dock. Antonio and Iggy start to unload the catch under surveillance of the two men left behind.

Pete Broderick sees his wife standing on the dock. He approaches her and wraps his arms around her, saying, "It was a good catch."

"What were all those Navy men doing on board your boat?" she asks.

Instead of keeping the U-boat incident from her, Pete decides to tell it all.

"Jesus, Mary, and Joseph, Peter Broderick, they could've killed all of you." Tears start to stream down her cheeks. "I won't say I told you so."

"You just did." He smiles and then kisses her cheek, tasting the salt in her tears. "Long as I did what I was told to do, we were not in any danger. The U-boat captain seemed okay and just wanted fish and water for his crew."

Elizabeth Ann holds her husband for a moment before she rushes aboard the trawler to hold her youngest son very close.

CHAPTER 22

Friday Afternoon
April 10, 1942

"A German submarine crew stealing fish from Pete's boat and it happens only sixty miles out at sea from here! This war is coming too near to us, Betty."

Gina Posada and Elizabeth Ann Broderick are at the Red Cross Center doing their weekly Friday afternoon volunteer duty. They're sitting at a long table with twelve other East Bay ladies, rolling bandages for an overseas shipment. Each donated a pint of blood earlier.

"It could've been worse, Gina. That U-boat captain might've sunk the *Elizabeth Ann*. That thought still makes me shiver. Needless to say, Ignatius will not be going on any other fishing trips with his dad."

"I asked Antonio to quit the *Elizabeth Ann*, Betty...fat chance of that ever happening."

"That new Coast Guard beach patrol commander has asked the boys to patrol on Friday nights so he can give his men liberty then. Ignatius wants to go there every Friday and his father has approved that. But with these German submarines coming so near to shore, I don't like it one bit, Gina."

"By the way, Betty, I met that new commander, Scott Lee, at the gas station. He's a charming Southern gentleman...and cute."

Elizabeth Ann laughs as she says, "Watch it, Gina. One East Bay woman's war time affair with a Coast Guard officer is quite enough."

"Not to worry about that, Betty. Antonio is as much man as I can handle. Wonder what's happening with Barbara Sheffield and her Coast Guard man. Will his absence make her heart grow even fonder?"

"Don't know about that, but her doctor husband seems to be pretty open with his hanky-panky. I saw him with Lois Cohen at the Oyster Shack sitting close while billing and cooing."

"How about Lois carrying on like that while her husband, Earnest, fights Japs on a Pacific island?"

"That island is Corregidor, Gina, and the newspapers say it's being attacked by the Japs."

Gina leaves the table with her arms full of rolled bandages to place in a shipping container. She returns with two cups of coffee and a small banner with a blue star on it. "Here, this is for you... the Red Cross supervisor is handing them out to mothers who have sons in the service to hang in their windows. I already have one."

Elizabeth Ann stares at the small swatch of silk cloth with a blue star sewn on it. Her thoughts go to the six East Bay mothers who have the same little banners hanging in their windows, only with gold stars on them instead of blue ones. She puts it in her purse and says, "Gina have you heard from Marcello?"

"I got a letter with some words inked out. They censor anything that might tell where he is. I think he's in England getting ready to go to North Africa."

"My Larry is still in training at San Diego. My guess is he'll be fighting on some of those Pacific islands occupied by the Japanese."

* * *

Barbara Sheffield is driving toward East Bay from Hyannis in her 1939 Chevrolet, a car that must last throughout the war years because automobile production has ceased. Since gas rationing commenced, there are no weekend tourists to clog the road as in peacetime, when it's filled with cars from Hyannis to Provincetown.

Barbara's thoughts go to the future, and reviewing her decision to become an RN, as she drives toward East Bay. *I've finished four weeks of training at the Cape Cod Hospital and adapted to it well. The course really is an accelerated one. In two weeks I'll be affiliating at a hospital in Boston. I'll not commute during that time, but will stay in a dorm at the hospital. On some weekends I'll be off and come home, unless I spend some time with Jane seeing the Boston sights.* The next thought brings a delightful tingle throughout her body. *Perhaps there'll be a chance for a trip to Charleston to visit Bill.*

Barbara reaches East Bay and pulls the Chevy into a parking space at the post office. She's anticipating a letter from Bill and when she opens the mailbox, there are two letters inside…one from Bill and one from her son Danny. Instead of reading them right away, she drives to a beach parking lot on the Atlantic side of the Cape, where the sun is starting to set. She parks the car and begins to read Danny's letter first.

Dear Mom,

How's your nurse's training going? I'm proud of you. Keep it up. Speaking of nurses, I've dated a few Navy ones in Honolulu…almost as pretty as you. We're getting ready for something big. Except for the flying and the nurses, the waiting around is boring. I've made 26 carrier takeoffs and landings since getting here and I'm becoming an expert. I like the weather, the guys, and my Hell Cat fighter. Oh, and the nurses, of course.

I like getting your letters. Tell Allie and Jane to write.
Love,
Danny

Barbara folds the letter from Dan and opens the one from Bill. As she starts to read it, two train tickets fall out of the fold onto her lap.

Dearest Barbara,

I'm missing you very much. I've been at sea a lot and have been given command of the USS *Roper. From what I've seen of Charleston, it seems like a city you'd like. So come visit me! The ship is in port every six days for provisioning. Very active patrols around here—I'll tell you about them when I see you. I'm glad I finally got into the war.*

Hope your hospital training is going well. When you're in Boston and off on a weekend, it would be great if you could visit here. Anyway, I've sent round-trip train tickets with this letter (Boston to Charleston and return). Wish it were only a one-way to Charleston. Maybe we can work something out along those lines soon. . .although it's more complicated for you than for me.

Say hello to Allie for me. Can't wait to see you.
All my love,
Bill

Barbara folds the letter and places it in her purse. She looks out at the ocean and the horizon beyond, where clouds have been colored red by a setting sun. Her thoughts go to Bill, her first real love. Then in a flash of anger, she thinks of her husband, who is openly carrying on an affair with Lois Cohen.

She recalls Clark Gable's words in the film *Gone With the Wind.* Barbara starts the Chevy engine and says out loud to an empty ocean, "Frankly. . .I don't give a damn."

THE DUNE

Friday Evening at Sunset

"These hot dogs sure taste good." Junie is smearing mustard and relish on his second one.

Iggy agrees. "Yeah, they're better than that horse meat my mom tried to serve last night...yuck. She said it's because of the war that there's a shortage of beef. My dad started whinnying like a horse and I couldn't stop laughing."

"Soon as it's dark, we've got a blackout rule on the beach, guys." Junie looks up at the ladder entrance. "We'll keep the ladder opening covered so no light can escape. That new stove pipe through the hole in the canvas roof will give us enough air."

"How about using our flashlights on the beach, Junie?"

"Allie, you can only use them in emergencies."

"Could be kinda scary, but the breaking surf is a white path to walk along," Iggy says.

"Nothing should scare you, Iggy, after that German U-boat attack."

"It wasn't really an attack, Junie, just a robbery."

"Whatever you want to call it, Iggy...it's still a scary thing for a kid."

"Yeah, but like I told you before, the U-boat captain seemed like a good guy. He gave me a fountain pen as a souvenir."

"A Nazi being a good guy, Iggy...I doubt it."

"Well, he..."

Iggy's retort is interrupted by the sound of the Coast Guard jeep pulling up beside the dune.

Lieutenant Commander Scott Lee pokes his head through the ladder opening and says, "Hey, how're my auxiliary sailors doing? Y'all ready to do your first night beach patrol?" He climbs down the ladder. "I thought y'all might like a little ol' taste of chocolate ice cream." He sets a bag with the ice cream down on an orange crate. "Man, you got all the comforts of home in this here dune...cots, sleeping bags, books, and even hot dogs cooking on a Sterno can."

"Thanks for the ice cream, sir," Junie says. "Would you like a hot dog, sir?"

"Don't mind if I do. But no more of the 'sir' stuff. Like I said, I'm Scott to y'all."

They sit on the cots. The boys spoon their ice cream while Scott munches on his hot dog and talks football to the boys.

"Oh, I almost forgot." Scott reaches in his pocket and hands Iggy the fountain pen given to him by Karl Heineke. "A Navy guy named Grogan dropped this off for you. They did their lab work on it and it's clean."

Allie and Junie inspect the pen and the insignia of the German Submarine Service stamped on it. A loud "wow" comes from both.

* * *

Junie Cohen and Allie Sheffield draw the first three-hour beach patrol Iggy will remain in the dune, monitoring the radio, until it's his turn to rotate with one of them. They've got it worked out so each boy will spend an equal time on patrol and get some sleep in between.

Junie and Allie walk along the surf toward Highland Light on their first leg of patrol. Even without a moon, the white surf and light-colored sand provide an outline for them to follow without a flashlight beam. Each boy is quiet in his own thoughts. The only sounds are the surf breaking and an occasional seagull screech until Junie speaks.

"Allie, I didn't want to mention this to you, but some kids in school are blabbing about it."

"You mean my mom and Bill Childs? I'm getting that stuff, too, Junie."

"That's not all of it, though, Allie. My mother and your dad…"

"Yeah, I know. And my dad….he's not hiding it. Goes to the Oyster Shack with your mom and they hold hands. It's kinda hard to hear about that from the kids at school who get it from their parents. My dad and your mom are together a lot at the office in our house." Allie picks up a rock and flings it out on the surf. "This frigging war has changed East Bay and our lives."

"Worse thing is my dad is fighting Japs on Corregidor and he doesn't have a clue that this is going on. It shits!"

"Funny thing, Junie, is they think we don't know about it."

"I think we should at least let them know that we know. What do you think?"

"That's hard to do." Allie kicks a clump of sand then says, "But I suppose we should. Hey, no matter what, we'll still be friends. Us dune guys stick together, Junie…right?"

"Yeah, like brothers or stepbrothers." He laughs at that thought and punches Allie on the arm as they turn away from Highland Light and patrol the beach toward Provincetown.

CHAPTER 23

At Sea, April 14, 1942
On Board U-432
Ninety-three Nautical Miles from Lorient, France

"The air in this boat is putrid, Hans."

"Yes, sir, I know, but after seventy-three days on patrol with forty-three men crammed into this metal tube and only one head—well, maybe that's why. There's also rotten food, along with those unwashed bodies and diesel fumes to add to the stale air, with very little ventilation to cleanse it. We can't expect this boat to smell like a perfumed French bordello, Karl."

Heineke and Hans are in the captain's nook having their lunch. It's the last of the fish chowder.

Heineke smiles at Hans's French bordello comparison and then asks, "What's the condition of the crew?"

"Well, Weisel's arm is going to need surgery to repair arm muscle when we dock. We have about eight men with dysentery. All of us are dehydrated, and the last of the water will be gone tonight."

Heineke's eyes narrow as he gives an order. "Hans, in the next ten hours before we dock, I want you to rotate five men every hour on deck watch so all of our crew can breathe some fresh air. And tell Fritz to radio this message to Kapitanleutnant Godt, the admiral's adjutant: Because of conditions aboard U-432, I respectfully request that no…repeat, no…ceremony be planned when we dock at Lorient. We have sick and injured crewmembers on board and wish to stand down."

In an hour, the reply from Godt comes back agreeing to eliminate the docking ceremonies except for the band. His message adds that 'there will be no standing in formation for the crew of U-boat *432*.' He ended it, "Great hunting, Heineke...Godt."

* * *

Ten hours later, they enter the harbor at Lorient. As they dock, the band plays the usual march music, with their standard, "Germany Over All." Four ambulances are standing by, ready to take Weisel and the most seriously ill to the hospital. The other members of the crew are at ease on the deck, where Heineke addresses them.

"Men, you've done a great job under trying conditions. Those of you who feel well enough, go to our Bistro Luis watering hole and drink plenty of cold water or beer." A cheer rises up from the crew after the word "beer."

"Now, help your sick comrades into those ambulances. They'll be sure to join you later."

Weisel is able to walk to an ambulance unaided. As he passes by Heineke, He raises his left hand in a salute and says, "Thank you, sir. I'll be back for the next patrol."

The only member of Admiral Dönitz's staff to come on board is Kapitanleutnant Godt. He approaches Heineke and says, "Kapitanleutnant, your patrol was a record one in tonnage: eight ships sunk for a total of fifty-seven thousand two hundred and twenty tons. Congratulations! Get some rest and put on a clean uniform tomorrow. The admiral wishes that you meet with him in his quarters for lunch at thirteen-hundred hours." Godt salutes him without following it with the customary stiff, arm-raising gesture in honor of the Führer and is quick to depart U-*432*.

"You've another audience with the admiral, Karl. Wonder what's up this time?"

Heineke looks at the damaged deck where the bomb hit and the hull pockmarked with bullet holes. "Maybe it's about bringing back one of his submarines with holes in it, Hans."

"I don't think this boat will be going out on patrol too soon, Karl. Wonder if I'll get a chance to go to Augsburg for a visit..."

"I'm sure that'll be arranged. Hang around for a day or so until I have an idea about what's next for U-432 and us."

"Good. Can't wait to see Ingrid and my three children, and have a Bavarian beer with Ingrid's wiener schnitzel dinner."

"I thought you might be looking forward to a bowl of her fish chowder instead, Hans."

Hans's laugh follows Heineke's when he says, "Never again will I crave that chowder after ten straight days of it."

* * *

Captain Heineke is the last to leave the U-432. He collects his personal belongings, including Marie Paul's picture, and puts them in a sea bag. Before climbing the ladder, he pauses to look through the boat. Even though the hatches have been open for over an hour, the acrid stench still persists.

On deck he encounters the structural engineer from the submarine maintenance division studying the hole made by the bomb. The engineer shakes his hand in greeting and says, "Good thing you didn't dive too deep, Captain." He points down at the jagged metal opening in the deck. "There are several cracks in the pressure hull that probably would've made it fail at great depth."

"When will you be able to get it fixed, Oberleutnant?" Heineke asks.

"That depends on how far the cracks penetrate into the pressure hull and how far they've spread, sir. The inspection alone will take a week—and the time for repair, if that's at all possible… who knows? In any case, this boat will not be ready for a sea patrol for at least a month, if ever. It must go into dry dock."

Before leaving, Heineke's eyes scan from bow to stern and he speculates that this could be his last look at U-432.

Later, in the officers' barracks, Heineke savors the steaming hot water shower that flows over his body for half an hour before he gets between clean white sheets and drops off to a sound sleep.

* * *

At noon, Heineke is aroused from a deep sleep by an orderly carrying his cleaned and pressed dress uniform on a hanger. He checks his watch… just enough time to make his appointment with Admiral Dönitz.

At 1300, Heineke is with the admiral in his private quarters, having lunch. It's his first real food in six weeks: a slab of roast beef with carrots, potatoes, and beets, accompanied by a dark red Merlot wine from a French vineyard. The admiral wants to know every detail related to each enemy action. He is especially interested in the U-432's attack by the aircraft.

"When did your men on watch report the aircraft?"

"According to them, sir, it was a speck on the horizon coming straight at the boat when they first saw it and reported it. It seems like the crew of that plane detected the U-432 before we saw them."

"Damn. The intelligence reports are correct…the Americans have perfected their *radio detection and ranging* device. They're calling it *radar*.

The fear of the submarine crew has always been an attack by aircraft before they can crash dive. Now, they've a device that will detect a U-boat well before those on watch can make a visual sighting."

"Sir, if I may, perhaps there's a way for a U-boat to capture that radio signal from the enemy aircraft and get an advance warning of the attack."

"Good, Heineke. I want you to brief our electronic engineers on that idea. Hopefully, they're already involved with a similar solution. Anyway, report your findings on their progress to me in a couple of days."

The admiral's eyelids narrow to a squint before he adds, "Now, Heineke, tell me about your encounter with the American fishing boat on Georges Bank."

"Well, sir, as you know, we missed our rendezvous with the milk cow and in order to obtain food and water I resorted to piracy."

"Yes, yes, I know that, but why didn't you destroy the radio on board?"

"The only answer I can give to that is a humanitarian one. The captain had his young son with him and offered no resistance. He cooperated completely. To smash a radio that he relied on for navigation and emergencies seemed a harsh act at the time. I thought I would be far away before he could radio my position. I was wrong."

"Very well, Heineke. I accept your excuse. Under those circumstances I may have done the same...don't let that get out to some of my bloodthirsty colleagues, though."

"Admiral, the U-432 will be out of commission for some time, according to the structural engineer. Will I receive another assignment?"

"I have the preliminary report on the condition of U-432. You will be in command of a new boat scheduled to arrive here from Kiev in two weeks. I'm sending you out on a special mission. I'll brief you on it when I have all the details from those involved."

They're finishing the lunch with coffee and a crème caramel dessert when Adjutant Godt interrupts. "Admiral, the Führer has called."

Admiral Dönitz excuses himself and says, "Stay, Heineke. I'll be back shortly."

The admiral returns to the table in ten minutes. He smiles and says, "That phone call from the Führer was about you. Seems like Herr Hitler has heard about the record amount of tonnage you've sunk and would like to personally award you with some leaves and swords to go with your Iron Cross. Because of your and some other U-boat captains' successes, Hitler has become a believer in Operation Drumbeat. We will both fly to the Wolf's Lair tomorrow morning. Be at the Aerodrome for takeoff at zero-six hundred hours."

Heineke's thought: *I'm proud to receive the medal, but coming face to face with Hitler whose dictatorship and rumored atrocities I abhor will be difficult.*

* * *

After leaving Admiral Dönitz's quarters, Heineke stops by Adjutant Godt's desk for his sealed orders; while there, he requests leave authorization for Hans Topp.

As Heineke walks down the main street of Lorient on his way to the officers' barracks, he passes near to Bistro Luis, the hangout for the U-432 crew. He has a hunch Hans might be inside and if so, he'll be able to give him his leave orders there. When Heineke enters the bistro he's greeted by a loud cheer followed by applause from the members of his crew. Hans is seated at the bar, sipping a large stein of beer.

"Looks like my crew is no longer dehydrated, Hans."

"We're working on it, Captain." He orders a beer for Heineke and then says, "We heard a rumor from headquarters that you're going to have some other hardware hanging on that Iron Cross."

"News travels fast." Heineke takes a sip of his beer. "Did you also hear that you're going on leave?"

"No, that news didn't travel as fast." A broad smile lights up Hans's face.

Heineke reaches in his tunic inside pocket and gives Hans the leave orders and train passes for Augsburg. "Your train leaves at zero-six hundred hours. We both have command performances to-morrow...yours in Augsburg and mine at the Wolf's Lair in East Prussia. After this beer, let's get some sleep so we'll be up for it, okay?"

Hans takes a large gulp from his stein to finish his beer and gets up from his barstool. Then both he and Heineke leave the bistro accompanied by good-natured boos and cat calls from the crew of U-432.

CHAPTER 24

April 17, 1942

The Junkers JU-52 taxies to the beginning of the runway at the Lorient Airdrome. The three engines rev-up to a scream as the plane starts to roll along the concrete surface until takeoff speed is achieved. The aircraft's special configuration includes a fabric covering the corrugated metal hull to dampen the engine noise. There's a galley and one flight attendant to serve the admiral and whoever accompanies him. The cabin is roomy since only ten of the original eighteen seats remain. Heineke and one other U-boat captain are the only passengers besides the admiral.

As the plane climbs to its cruising altitude, Heineke's thoughts range from not looking forward to a meeting with the head of the Nazi party—a regime he has grown to loathe—to wishing there were a way to spend some time with Marie Paul before going off on that *special mission* the admiral mentioned.

The flight to East Prussia will take six hours with a stop in Berlin for fuel. Admiral Dönitz brought a leather briefcase on board the aircraft, filled with paperwork, and he remains busy working his way through it. Coffee with a croissant is served by the male flight attendant. Kapitanleutenant Wolfgang Wattenberg, who will also be decorated by Hitler, and Heineke engage in U-boat talk as the tri-motor aircraft drones along on its course toward Berlin.

* * *

As Admiral Dönitz's Junkers JU-52 makes its way toward Berlin, Lancaster bombers take off from an airfield at Waddington, England. They don't have a fighter escort on this mission. Each bomber has been fueled with two thousand one hundred and four gallons of petrol for the two thousand-mile round trip to the target and back. They're loaded with four one thousand-pound high explosive bombs, fitted with eleven-second delay detonators. The Lancasters set a course for Augsburg, Germany. Their target is a diesel engine factory there.

* * *

Hans Topp fell asleep soon after he boarded the second leg of his train journey to Augsburg at the Montparnasse station in Paris. Four hours later, he's jolted awake when the train makes a sudden stop. He looks out the window and sees a forested landscape without any buildings to indicate the train's approach into Augsburg. Soon the conductor passes through the car, informing passengers that they're ten miles from Augsburg and being held up because of an air raid on the city. Hans's heart starts to beat faster as his thoughts go to Ingrid and the kids. *It's the first air raid on Augsburg. I wanted them out of the city before that happened.*

One hundred and twenty miles from Augsburg, the group of Lancasters is jumped by a flight of *Bf 109s*. The German fighters wreak havoc on the unescorted formation and four Lancasters go down in flames. Luckily, the *Bf 109s* are forced to withdraw for lack of fuel before they can cause any more losses. The remaining two Lancasters fly straight toward the diesel engine factory target at tree-top level. The ground defenses are firing at them and the flak is thick. They begin their run out and then pull away from the scene to set a course for the return journey. Only two of their thousand-pound bombs are direct hits on the diesel engine factory; the other six fall on an adjacent residential area.

* * *

After an hour, the train gets its clearance to proceed into the station. Hans becomes more apprehensive when it reaches the outskirts of Augsburg. He sees smoke billowing from an area of the city in which his apartment is located. It seems longer to Hans than the fifteen minutes it takes the train to reach the station and stop. He rushes out of the building, hails a taxi, and tells the driver the address of his apartment.

The taxi driver says, "I can't take you all the way there, sir. It's blocked off because of the bombing. Only emergency vehicles are allowed into that area."

Hans's anxiety increases even more as he screams at the driver, "Then fucking take me as close as you can get."

He's let out of the taxi five blocks from his apartment, where barriers have been placed to block the street. Hans runs down the street to where his apartment should have been and finds only a pile of smoldering rubble there. He approaches a fireman and says, "My wife and children live in number 29. Are they…?"

The fireman shakes his head and says, "All in the building have perished. There was a woman and three children, identified as Topp. They were buried in the bricks…they're gone. No time for them to get to a bomb shelter. The bombers came in low and fast. I'm very sorry, Oberleutenant."

Hans's scream echoes through a street filled with tumbled red bricks from buildings not intended as targets. He shakes his fist at the sky and yells, "You bastards!"

CHAPTER 25

The Junkers JU-52 touches down at Rastenburg Airport, five miles from the Wolf's Lair. A staff car is waiting on the tarmac. They pass through three heavily guarded checkpoints with armored vehicles and tanks positioned at places in between. They then enter the Wolf's Lair complex, made up of thick reinforced concrete bunkers. The car stops at one of the largest and they get out.

Heineke and Wattenberg are led into a large hall to join several Air Force and Army men who will also receive medals. Admiral Dönitz leaves them and enters a room off to the side of the hall. He's been told that the Führer wants to have a private word with him. Heineke recognizes Goring and Jodl among a group of Hitler's staff seated in front of them. The flags of the Third Reich are in place around the hall and an orchestra is seated to the left.

After ten minutes of waiting, Heineke sees the door that Admiral Dönitz had entered open and Adolph Hitler struts into the hall, followed by the admiral. All stand and the seven men who will receive medals form a line. The orchestra plays a march before Hitler starts down the line to award the medals.

Heineke waits at attention with the others to receive his Iron Cross with oak leaves and swords. As Hitler comes down the line to approach him his nervousness turns to a revulsion that makes his stomach churn and his heart beat faster. Heineke notices that the Fuehrer spends time chatting with each man before the medal is presented. Heineke is the fourth in line to receive his. He thinks: *I hope he doesn't talk to me very long.*

In his peripheral vision Heineke starts to get a close look at the leader of the Third Reich...*He's much like the photograph hanging in all the U-boats: black hair combed to fall down on one side of his forehead and telltale abbreviated mustache. He is wearing a tan civilian suit that's modified to appear as a uniform, like no other one in all of his military.*

The third man in line is an air force pilot who has shot down fifty-two enemy planes. Hitler asks him to tell about his last victory. The pilot obliges, using his hands to describe the dog fight, and Hitler is delighted by that charade. After the pilot is presented his medal, he salutes his Führer with an outstretched hand and says, "Heil Hitler."

Heineke thinks: *Shit, I can't do that Heil Hitler salute of adoration for a man I despise.* His apprehensions increase as Hitler comes closer to him.

When it's Heineke's turn to be presented his medal, Hitler stands before him, smiles, and says, "So this is my U-boat commander who robs an American fishing boat of their fish."

"Yes, sir. We were out of food and water and that fish saved us from starvation."

"And Kapitanleutnant Heineke, you have set a record of tonnage in your eight patrols. Also, you saved a crewmember on the deck of your U-boat while being attacked by an American aircraft. I award you the Iron Cross with swords and oak leaves." With those words, he hangs the medal around Heineke's neck and says, "Please enjoy your meal today with the other heroes of the Third Reich." Hitler then pauses like he's anticipating the usual salute. When it doesn't come he stares with a blank expression at Heineke for five seconds, until...

Heineke tries to avoid the "heil Hitler" salute by saying, "I'll enjoy the meal, sir, if it's not fish chowder."

Hitler's stern look turns to a smile… his laugh then became loud and boisterous, almost maniacal, as he moves on to the next man in line.

* * *

After a meal of wild boar and a white wine from the Mosel River region, they enter the staff car for the ride back to the airfield at Rastenburg. Heineke again notes the fortifications and the three checkpoints and has a thought: *If at some point this war under Hitler's command degrades, it would be a very difficult to remove him in a covert operation from this fortress.*

Before they arrive at the airfield, Admiral Dönitz turns to Heineke and Wattenberg and says, "That private talk I had with the Führer before the ceremony was about two things. He has concern that commando raids from England to the coast of France could occur and wants me to plan a move of the submarine headquarters from Lorient to Paris. So, we fly to Paris from here. I need two days to look for an appropriate place for the headquarters." He smiles at Heineke. "I believe you have a lady friend in Paris, Heineke, and won't mind a delay in getting back to Lorient…only this time please wear your uniform and speak German instead of English."

Then the admiral looks over at Wattenberg and says, "I'm sure a single man, as you are, will find something to enjoy in Paris for a couple of days. Of course, you both have another option…that is to take the train from Paris today back to Lorient." His smile at them is a broad one.

In unison, the two submarine captains agree to the layover in Paris.

"Very well, then we'll depart Orly Field at zero-seven hundred on Monday. Now, the second subject Hitler discussed with me is the special mission I spoke to you about earlier, Heineke. It's one of his pet projects and he wants the principals involved that are now in training to meet at Lorient on Friday, May 1, to formulate a plan for your mission. Before your new U-boat arrives from Kiev, I'd like you to meet with the engineers to see what they've done to counter this new radar device the enemy has on their aircraft."

CHAPTER 26

Heineke and Wattenberg depart Orly Field by taxi for the city. Admiral Dönitz leaves in a chauffeured staff car for Versailles, where a meeting relating to the move of submarine headquarters is to be held.

The taxi maneuvers slowly down the Champs Elysees while both men enjoy the sights of an occupied and peaceful, not war-torn, Paris—a reprieve for both from that ocean conflict to which they must soon return.

As the taxi crosses over the Seine and starts to proceed down Boulevard Saint-Germaine toward the Left Bank, it's stopped by a traffic jam. The cause is a group of men and women being loaded onto a German Army truck by French police. They each have yellow stars on their sweaters, blouses, and coats.

Heineke asks the driver, "What's going on?"

The driver answers with one word: "Jews."

Heineke shrugs his shoulders and looks over at Wattenberg.

"I'm not sure of this, but I've heard rumors," Wattenberg says.

Heineke spies an SS officer standing on the sidewalk, observing the scene from a distance. He leaves the taxi and approaches him, saying, "Oberleutnant, what's going on here?"

The officer salutes him and says, "Jews."

Put off by the same one-word answer he got from the taxi driver, he asks, "Where are they being taken?"

"To Poland by train to a camp called Auschwitz."

"What's their crime?"

"Just being Jewish, sir."

"Who ordered this?"

"The Gestapo did."

"Why aren't these arrests being carried out by Germans instead of French police?"

"Those are my orders, sir."

Heineke returns to the taxi as the fully loaded truck with its human cargo leaves for the train station.

He says to Wolfgang Wattenberg, "Guess I've been at sea too long to hear any rumors. What have you heard?"

"Well, I hear that there's a program initiated by Hitler to eliminate the Jewish population. They call it: *the final solution.*"

Heineke shakes his head. With a sharp look at the blond, blue-eyed Wattenberg, he says, "That's criminal...we'll all be hanged because of it."

Wattenberg's response is silence accompanied by a blank stare at Heineke.

Wattenberg leaves the taxi near Ile Saint Louis with a fast handshake followed by a "heil Hitler" salute that doesn't get a return from Heineke.

The taxi continues on until it stops at the Brasserie Albert, where Heineke pays the fare and enters the building. Albert Chabot greets him. The white-haired owner recognizes him immediately on this visit and happily bestows on Karl a hug with a kiss on both cheeks. It's late afternoon and the brasserie is empty of patrons. Heineke is ushered to his favorite table by the window, where Albert removes his signature green apron, joins Heineke, and calls the waiter to order a special wine from his cellar.

"How are things with you, Albert?" Heineke asks.

Albert looks around the empty room as if by habit before answering in a whisper, "The mood of the German military here is changing. They've gone from being glorious and boisterous conquerors to cruel and sometimes vicious occupiers of Paris. Maybe it's a feeling that they could lose this war…since the Americans have joined it, there's the fear of an invasion. Lately, they've been taking out those feelings, especially on the Jews."

"I saw some of that on the way here, Albert, and I'm having a problem understanding the reason behind this purge. Why are the French police making the arrests instead of the SS?"

"I'm not sure of this, but the rounding up of Jews by our police may be a strategy to involve France in something that may come later on that's worse than just being held in a camp."

Karl Heineke takes a sip of wine and then shakes his head as Albert's innuendo brings a horrific thought to his mind, adding to the distressing circumstances prompted by Wattenberg's *final solution* rumor. He changes the subject. "How's your business doing, Albert?"

"It's strange, but my German military clientele are drinking more than ever. They could be trying to drown their fear." He pours some wine from a bottle of vintage Merlot into both glasses. "And how does the war go with you, Karl?"

"I have a good leader…an admiral who looks after his men and doesn't flaunt any Nazism. We are successful to this point. I've just received an Iron Cross with swords and oak leaves, but, Albert, I just want it all to end."

They talk for another hour until Heineke leaves to take his devious route through the back alley behind Boulevard Saint-Germaine to Marie Paul's apartment.

* * *

"Do you want me to have a heart attack with these surprise visits of yours, Karl?" Marie Paul asks this in English after he knocked on the door, entered the apartment, and gathered her in his arms.

He explains the reason for the unexpected trip to Paris and then holds her in a long embrace. She breaks away from it to say, "I have a visitor, Karl. Come, I'll introduce you to her."

She takes him by the hand and leads him to the living room, where a little dark-haired girl with big brown eyes is sitting on the sofa clutching a rag doll. "Gretchen Schwartz, I'd like you to meet Karl Heineke."

Gretchen looks his uniform up and down and holds the doll tighter as if fearing this German officer.

"No, no, little one, he is my friend and will soon be yours," Marie Paul says.

Heineke approaches Gretchen and drops down on one knee. "What's your doll's name, Gretchen?"

She hesitates for a moment and then says, "Anne."

"That's a nice name. May I shake her hand?"

She pauses at first before offering the doll's arm to Heineke.

"Now, may I shake your hand, Gretchen?"

She's reluctant at first, but then slowly offers her hand.

He takes it in his and says, "I'm Karl. How old are you?"

"I'm almost six."

"Well, I'm almost thirty-one, Gretchen."

She smiles and says, "Wow!"

Later, Marie Paul explains the reason for her visitor. "She's the daughter of a Jewish professor at the Sorbonne. He fears that with his wife he'll soon be rounded up and taken to a camp, so he asked that I hide Gretchen, his only child, because he's heard rumors that the Jewish children will also be encamped soon."

"How can I help?" Heineke asks.

"Well, my darling, you may help by going to the brasserie to-night until eleven. My brother and another man from the Resistance are coming to take Gretchen to Normandy, where my parents will hide her on their farm until this stupid war is over. So, it's best that you not be here when they arrive. But come back to me after. I'll have a warm bed waiting."

Heineke spends the evening at Brasserie Albert. Later, he returns to the apartment, undresses, and slips into the bed beside a naked Marie Paul. She wakes up, turns, and moves into his waiting arms.

In the morning, during breakfast, Marie Paul shows Karl a photograph of her parents' farm in Normandy. She hands him a slip of paper noting the town and location, saying, "I want you to promise to try to make your way there if the Allies invade and it looks as if Germany is losing the war. My brother has some information on an invasion that may come to the Normandy beaches and he'll help you get to the farm, if it's at all possible."

Karl takes the slip of paper with the directions to the farm and tucks it in his wallet. His thoughts about Germany losing the war are conflicting ones.

Heineke remains in the apartment until early Monday morning, when he leaves for Orly and the flight back to Lorient.

Eastern Sea Frontier

Enemy Action Diary

April 21, 1942
1630 hours

Army bomber saw diesel smoke an oil slick at 41-12N, 70-50W. Possibly from sub. Position 8 miles south of Martha's Vineyard, Cape Cod.

CHAPTER 27

East Bay, April 24, 1942

Iggy hurt his finger in a basketball game during gym period. He thinks it might be broken so, after school, while the boys are on their way home, they stop at Kline's Shoe Store on Main Street to check it out. They get permission to use the shoe-fitting X-ray device. Iggy places his hand in the slot where new shoes on a customer's shod feet would be inserted to check for a proper fit. Iggy can't see the skeletal bones of his left hand because he is at foot level, below the device, but Junie makes the reading from the display above.

"It's not broken, Iggy, just a sprain."

After that fast diagnosis, they leave Kline's and continue down Main Street toward each of their homes.

"See you guys tonight at the dune," Junie says as he leaves Iggy and Allie to run across Main Street toward his house. When he sees a Western Union messenger's car in the driveway, his worry begins. Junie's anxiety mounts to fear when he hears a scream come from inside the house.

The messenger passes him with his head down as Junie rushes to the front door and into the house. "Is it Dad, Mom?"

She sobs a reply that sounds like 'yes' and hands a telegram to Junie. He starts to read it.

WESTERN UNION

WASHINGTON, D.C., APRIL 23, 1942

MRS. EARNEST S. COHEN
102 Main Street, East Bay, Massachusetts

THE DEPARTMENT OF THE ARMY DEEPLY REGRETS
TO INFORM YOU THAT YOUR HUSBAND, EARNEST
SAMUEL COHEN, CAPTAIN U.S. ARMY, WAS KILLED IN
ACTION WHILE IN THE SERVICE OF HIS COUNTRY.
THE DEPARTMENT EXTENDS TO YOU ITS SINCEREST
SYMPATHY IN YOUR GREAT LOSS. NO INFORMATION
IS AVAILABLE AT PRESENT IN REGARD TO DISPOSI-
TION OF THE REMAINS...

Junie stops reading the telegram at that point and looks hard
at his mother, who's still sobbing. The telegram is shaking in his
hands, but he's not crying. His pent-up rage about his mother's affair erupts. He throws the telegram to the floor and shouts, "Now
you can marry Dr Sheffield!"

"Oh, my God...you know?" More tears stream down Lois Cohen's face.

"Mom, the whole town knows," Junie says before rushing out
of the house and heading for the dune.

* * *

Elizabeth Ann Broderick and Gina Posada are at the Red Cross
Center for their Friday afternoon volunteer work. They're sitting at the
long table with the other women cutting and rolling bandages. The

head Red Cross lady approaches the table and says, "I just heard that Earnest Cohen has been killed in action on Corregidor. I sent several of our ladies to the Cohen house to see if we could be of any assistance." As she leaves the table, she adds, " I thought you'd like to know."

Gina and Elizabeth Ann stare a long time at each other before speaking. Another East Bay man killed in action brings a mixture of thoughts to their minds. At first they think about their own son's vulnerability in combat, and then sympathetic thoughts turn toward Lois Cohen and her son. And, lastly, each wonders about the impact this sad news will have on the affair between Dr. Sheffield and Lois, as well as the situation between Bill Childs and Barbara Sheffield.

Gina speaks first: "Betty, I'm shaken by this news. Every time I hear of another East Bay person killed in this war, my fear for Marcello increases."

"I feel the same way about Larry, Gina." She finishes rolling a bandage and says, "It's a terrible tragedy for Lois and Junie, but that affair makes everything much worse for Lois. Allie Sheffield is staying at our house Saturday with Ignatius. Barbara is in Boston for the weekend."

* * *

As Gina and Elizabeth Ann roll their last bandages, Barbara Sheffield is at South Station in Boston getting ready to board a train to New York with a change there for Charleston, South Carolina. Reluctantly, she enters a phone booth to call home. After two rings, the doctor answers. She tells him that she'll not be home until next weekend and that Allie will sleep over at the Brodericks'.

"Barbara, I have some sad news." There's a pause before he continues. "Earnest Cohen has been killed in action."

She remains silent for a moment to let the news sink in then says, "Does that complicate your affair with Lois?"

She hears what sounds like a cough before he asks, "You know?"

"Yes, Raymond. I wasn't the last to know, like the proverbial saying goes."

The phone is silent for ten seconds until Barbara says, "I have a train to catch. I'm on my way to Charleston, South Carolina, for the weekend."

"Is it Childs?" he asks.

She says, "Yes," and then places the phone in its cradle.

Barbara hurriedly passes through South Station on her way to her train track. The station is filled with soldiers, sailors, and marines. When she reaches Grand Central Station in New York to change trains, the scene is the same: Men as young as, and younger than, her Danny are going off to war.

* * *

Bill's there to meet her at the train station in Charleston the next morning. When she rushes to him, he wraps his arms around her and holds her before a word is said. She feels this man's love, a sensation she's always wanted.

The Dune

Instead of riding his bike, Junie decides to walk down Shore Road to the dune. He needs time to try to clear his head. He thinks it's weird that he doesn't cry about his dad.

Halfway there, a Coast Guard jeep pulls up beside him. Scott Lee asks, "Need a ride, Junie? Hop in. You've had a rough day. Sorry about your dad. From what I hear through my grapevine sources, the fight defending Corregidor was a valiant one."

Those words burst a dam and Junie's tears release in deep sobbing.

"Hey, that's okay, partner. Let it go and don't hold back any longer."

"But my mom...I..."

"I know, but don't be too hard on her. She needs you now."

"But she..."

Scott interrupts him. "Difficult to understand right now for you, but those things between men and women happen, especially during war time."

Another deep sob comes from Junie before he says, "I guess you know about them?"

"Yes, I do. Let's get on to the dune, where your friends are waiting to start the Friday night patrol."

Allie and Iggy are waiting for him. They both say it at almost at the same time: "Sorry to hear about your dad."

That starts another bit of sobbing by Junie until Allie hands him a mug of hot chocolate and, as an afterthought, his cherished medical dictionary from a slot in the orange crate. He presents it to Junie with a laugh and is joined by Iggy's giggle.

Junie says, "You bastards." His sob turns to laughter and soon after that they plan their Friday night beach patrol.

It's Allie and Junie on the first patrol with Iggy manning the dune control center.

They start out toward Highland Light; both are quiet until Junie breaks their silence. "Well, my mom knows that I know about it now."

"Yeah, so does my dad."

"You told him that you know, Allie?"

"Not exactly...he told me that my mom was going to South Carolina to be with Bill Childs this weekend."

"How did you handle that?"

"I said, 'You brought that on' then he slapped me in the face and I left for the dune."

"Jesus, I blame the Japs for this crap...if they hadn't bombed Pearl Harbor, none of this shit would've happened." After saying those heartfelt words, Junie scales a flat rock as hard as he can out onto the breaking surf.

At 7:00 p.m., after an hour patrolling the stretch toward Provincetown, they see lights and bright flashes far out to sea. They report it to Iggy, who radios the sighting to the Coast Guard duty officer at Highland Light. Later on, at quarter to eleven, they observe and report that same activity out toward Nantucket Island.

Eastern Sea Frontier

Enemy Action Diary

April 24, 1942
1900 hours: Sub sighted by Army bomber at 1830 at 40-18 N, 68-25 W, which dropped three depth charges. No results observed. Position is 60 miles East of Nantucket Shoals Light.

2245 hours: U.S.S CORRY and U.S.S. BUCHANAN made good sound contact at 40-32 N., 69 50 W. and released a full barrage (. . .) 10 miles west of Nantucket Shoals Light.

April 26
0710 hours: Army bomber sighted periscope at 41-54 N, 69-20 W, 28 miles east of Nauset Beach, Cape Cod. Kept under continuous surveillance until 1822 hours.

CHAPTER 28

Lorient, France
May 1, 1942

"Hans, I need you with me at a meeting this afternoon at headquarters. They're going to discuss a special mission for us."

Heineke has finally located his executive officer after a search of the bistros and bars of Lorient.

Hans Topp is seated at the bar of an out-of-the-way brasserie not frequented by the submarine crews. He looks up at Heineke with bloodshot eyes and his words slur. "I can't."

"Listen to me, Hans." Heineke puts a hand on Hans's shoulder and gives him a look that demands attention. "I have not reported you as being absent without leave yet. I know how hard your loss is and I'm saddened by it, but the best thing for you is to stop drinking and return to duty."

"Jesus, Karl, they're all gone!" Tears stream down Hans's face for the first time since he accepted the news that his wife and children are dead. Before that, his thoughts of anger and sorrow were muddled by an alcohol-induced haze.

"Okay, Hans. Here's what we're going to do. You're going to leave this dive with me. We've got five hours before the meeting. You will come with me to the officers' barracks, where you'll shower, sober up, get something to eat, and then get into a fresh uniform."

Heineke pays the large bar bill. He helps his friend out the door of the brasserie and into a waiting military vehicle with a crewmember from U-432 behind the wheel.

* * *

Before the meeting, Admiral Dönitz beckons to Hans Topp and leads him into a side room; he's there for ten minutes.

The meeting starts at 3 p.m. sharp, in the map room with the admiral's adjutant, Kapitanleutnant Godt, introducing the members of the intelligence agency involved in the mission to Admiral Dönitz, Heineke, and Hans. Dressed in civilian clothes, the key players are Hermann Berger and Werner Haupt, who are fluent in the English language. They are the saboteurs that will be landed on the East Coast of the United States by a U-boat under the command of Heineke. Berger addresses the group. He's twenty-eight years old, tall, and muscular, with a short blond brush cut. He's wearing a dark suit and black shirt with a black tie. He has piercing steel-gray eyes that fix and hold contact for a few seconds on each man as he starts to present the plan.

"This mission is of the highest priority. It has been ordered by the Führer, who is very disturbed about the high rate of ship-building capability in America to make up for the losses imposed by the admiral's U-boats." He grins toward Admiral Dönitz and then continues. "After landing, we will join forces with a spy ring presently operating in the United States. We will split into two teams. One team will infiltrate a large ship-building plant in Quincy, Massachusetts, and slow their production rate by executing some of my ingenious sabotage plans." Berger's eyes narrow as he looks around the room for a reaction to his arrogant claim.

Hans Topp, sitting beside Heineke, nudges him with an elbow.

Berger continues, "The second team will block the Cape Cod Canal by sinking a ship there with a high explosive charge." Then he pauses to look at Heineke. "Kapitanleutnant Heineke, you are responsible for getting us to the landing spot at three in the morning on Saturday, May 30. I've selected this date and time because there's no moonlight then. I understand that you've been provided with a new U-boat to do so. I must remind you that this mission has priority over seeking and torpedoing any ships on the way to our launch site. Do you understand me?"

Before he answers Berger's belligerent-sounding question, Heineke looks over at Admiral Dönitz and sees an eyebrow rise up in reaction to Berger's comment. Heineke waits for the admiral's response.

"Now, Heineke, the U-boat will proceed directly from Lorient to the landing location," Admiral Dönitz says. "This mission has the highest level of scrutiny, including from the Führer. Your U-boat will avoid all enemy actions until after the men are launched."

Berger's smile is directed at Heineke, but it looks more like a smirk to him. Berger says, "Now, for the specifics about that launch location, I'll turn the presentation over to Werner Haupt. Heil Hitler!"

Haupt takes a wooden pointer and saunters toward the wall, where Godt pulls down a map of Cape Cod. Werner Haupt's manner is casual in contrast to that of Berger's. He's wearing baggy brown corduroy pants and a plaid shirt with a corncob pipe sticking out of a shirt pocket. His light brown hair is longer than a regulation military cut and he's sporting a thick brown mustache.

Werner Haupt places his pointer on the map of Cape Cod. "Here's where we'll land on May 30. According to intelligence reports, the beach along here is not patrolled because the Americans are lacking manpower in their Coast Guard." He slides the pointer six inches along the shoreline and says, "There's a lighthouse two kilometers south of this spot called Highland Light. People from the remnants of the Duquesne spy ring, thought to have been all rounded up by the FBI in 1941, will meet us here by car after we land." His pointer moves inland and touches down on Shore Road,

East Bay. "It's only a two hundred-meter walk to get there from our landing spot on the beach."

Werner sits and Berger stands up. "Are there any questions?"

Heineke asks a question addressed to Admiral Dönitz. "Sir, are my orders not to engage targets of opportunity?"

Berger answers, "Those are the orders I just gave you, Heineke."

The admiral raises his hand and says, "Now, wait a minute, Berger...please remember that Kapitanleutnant Heineke will command his boat and you are a passenger. Karl, as I said before, you'll proceed directly to the landing point from Lorient and engage shipping only after you offload Berger and Haupt. That's an order."

Berger's smirk reaches Heineke again and he asks, "Are there any more questions?" There's a pause, with none coming. "Alright, gentlemen, this mission is top-secret. The information we gave you is not to leave this room." He gives Heineke his steely, gray-eyed stare and says, "Heineke, you're not to tell your crew about the purpose of this mission and our destination. Is that understood?"

Heineke stares back at him and nods his head slowly up and down.

* * *

Later, Heineke and Hans are sitting in a booth in Bistro Luis, discussing the mission as well as their feelings about Berger and Haupt.

"Berger is going to be trouble," Hans says.

"Yeah, he did come on strong and is full of his Nazism. I'm sure I'll have to remind him from time to time who's in charge of the boat."

"The other spook, Haupt, seemed like an easygoing bloke. How about that corncob pipe, Karl?"

"Yeah, seems strange that he'd turn on his country. Before the meeting started, I had a chat with Werner in English, during which he spoke with an American Southern accent. He told me that he'd graduated from Wake Forest in Winston Salem, North Carolina, with a degree in electrical engineering. His father was an engineer with Western Electric there, became a citizen, and married his mother, an American. They divorced and his father returned to Germany. Werner visited him in 1938 and stayed too long. He was recruited by German intelligence and trained in espionage because of his fluency in English."

Hans takes a sip from his beer, shrugs his shoulders, and says, "I still think it's strange that he'd spy on his native country for the SS."

"Yeah, perhaps the methods of recruiting Haupt were typical of the SS and Gestapo. They have a way of holding something over one's head. Anyway, his having an electrical engineering background provides the basis for his expertise in the sophisticated explosive detonation devices important to his mission."

They both order ham and cheese in a freshly baked baguette, accompanied by another pint of beer. Heineke takes a bite of his sandwich, finishes chewing it, sips some beer, and asks, "How are you doing, my friend?"

"I'm feeling more human now. I'll never get over losing them all." Hans's eyes tear up before he says, "Thanks for getting me back to work. By the way, Admiral Dönitz called me aside before the meeting to express his condolences. He also asked if I wanted to take some time away from sea duty at that rest-and-recuperation place in the Alps. I refused his offer and told him I'd be better off returning to duty. When do we sail for Cape Cod?"

"We leave on May 19 in our new boat, U-582. We've got plenty of time for sea trials, provisioning, and training with the saboteurs before we go."

"That new boat will smell much better than old U-432 for awhile. And, Karl, we'll have some time for the crew to get used to having Berger around us in close quarters."

CHAPTER 29

East Bay, May 15, 1942

"Betty, have you heard from your son Larry?"

"Nothing lately, but I know the First Marine Division will start taking back those Pacific islands from the Japs soon and he'll be part of it."

It's Friday evening and Elizabeth Ann Broderick and Gina Posada are having dinner at the Oyster Shack after rolling bandages at the Red Cross Center.

"This is a nice change…with Pete and Antonio gone fishing and Ignatius patrolling the dune, there's no cooking dinner for the men. They have a hamburger special here tonight and I've been eating seafood for too long." Elizabeth Ann takes a sip of her Manhattan cocktail and asks, "Do you have any news on Marcello, Gina?"

"He's still in England. I got one of those victory letters from him that looks like they're written on tissue paper again, and much of it was censored with sentences and words blacked out."

"Wonder how Lois Cohen is doing?"

"I heard through the grapevine that she took a week off after that terrible telegram, but she's back at work with the doctor," Gina said.

"Both kids, Junie Cohen and Allie Sheffield, now know about what's going on with their parents."

"How do you know that, Betty?"

"They confided that to Ignatius and he told me. Those three kids are very close and there're no secrets kept among them. That's not all, Gina. Barbara and the doctor are now separated…at least in their house. According to Ignatius, Allie and his mother stay on

161

one side of the house when she's home and the doctor has arranged living quarters on the other side."

"Probably only a matter of time before Barbara divorces the doctor and marries Bill Childs."

Also, until this war ends, Bill's situation is up in the air."

Gina smiles and says, "Or out to sea."

The Dune, *Friday Evening*

"Not sure I'm gonna like these nighttime patrols."

"Hey, Iggy, there's a full moon tonight and it's almost bright as day."

"Yeah, but will every Friday night be this bright, Junie?"

"Well, anyway, last Saturday the government passed a law that makes daylight savings time last all year during the war," Allie says. "All the clocks went an hour ahead so it'll be lighter here for a longer time on Fridays."

They're eating cheese sandwiches plastered with yellow mustard and sipping Cokes before starting their patrol.

"Boogieman's not going to get you, Iggy." Allie then finishes chewing a big bite from his sandwich and says, "I got some news. My brother, Danny, wrote a letter from Hawaii. His carrier is back for repairs after being in the Battle of the Coral Sea. And guess what? He shot down three Jap planes...two more and he's an ace."

"Wow, I still want to fly fighter planes. Can't wait to graduate and join the..." Junie is interrupted by the sound of a Coast Guard jeep pulling up outside the dune.

Lt. Commander Scott Lee climbs down the ladder and says, "How y'all doing?" He takes a seat on one of the cots. "Got some news...y'all will be retiring from this man's Coast Guard Auxiliary on June 1, 1942. Ol' Coast Guard has finally got up to speed and we've got some manpower for patrolling this beach now. So in two weeks from now, you're relieved."

The news takes some time to register with the boys, but their concern is unified and Junie voices it. "Do we have to leave the beach and close up the dune, Scott?"

"Nah, y'all can stay, but not in an official capacity."

They're relieved by Scott's words. "Good," Junie says. "The summer's coming and the blue fish and stripers will be running."

"Y'all did a great job here and the Coast Guard's going to gin up some certificates for each of you that'll say that." Scott gets up from the cot and extends a handshake to each boy. As he climbs the ladder to leave, he turns and says, "I'll be looking forward to a fish fry here when y'all catch a mess of blues, stripers, or flounder. I'll bring the 'hush puppies.'"

They hear the jeep leave and Iggy says, "What the hell is a hush puppy?"

Junie answers the question with a shoulder shrug. "My guess is that it must be a Southern food of some kind."

Allie and Iggy leave the dune for their patrol. A full moon plays its light on the sand and water as they split up, Allie toward Provincetown and Iggy in the direction of Highland Light.

East Bay Harbor, Aboard the Elizabeth Ann

The trawler is headed out to sea on the Friday evening high tide. Pete Broderick is at the wheel, steering the *Elizabeth Ann* through the harbor. Antonio Posada is on deck, oiling a winch pulley. This trip will be a long one as they fish the Grand Banks.

"Hey, Antonio, come on up here...the coffee has perked."

Antonio finishes oiling, stows the oil can, and joins his captain in the wheelhouse.

Antonio pours two cups. The coffee is black and steaming, and he hands one of them to Pete as the trawler leaves the harbor and is put on a compass heading for the Grand Banks. He makes a toasting motion with his cup toward Pete's and says, "Here's to a good catch with no more robberies by a U-boat."

"The U-boats may've had their run, Antonio. I had a talk with that First Naval guy, Captain Johnson."

"That the same one who met us at the dock after the run-in with that U-boat, Pete?"

"Yeah, he finally came by for my signature on the incident report and said they've decided at the highest naval command on a new strategy to cut down our shipping losses by U-boats."

"What're they going to do?"

"Since January this year, ships have left the ports of Boston, New York, Charleston, Galveston, and the like alone, heading for Halifax, Nova Scotia, to be staged in convoys with a bunch of others before crossing the Atlantic to England and Russia. The German U-boats have had a field day seeking out these single ships and torpedoing them before they reach Halifax. Our losses were awful high."

"What'll happen now, Pete?"

"From now on they'll start out in our ports in convoys of as many as twenty ships escorted by Navy destroyers and Coast Guard cutters. No more single ships headed for Halifax as easy targets for torpedoes."

"Sounds like a good plan, Cap. Maybe they should've done it sooner."

Peter nods his head in agreement and takes a sip from his coffee cup. He looks past the bow of the trawler at a moonlit ocean and advances his throttle a couple of notches to increase the speed of the *Elizabeth Ann.*

CHAPTER 30

Lorient, France, May 15, 1942

"Well, Hans, four more days and we sail. I'm glad that training phase is over."

They're on the deck of U-582, monitoring the loading of provisions down below.

"Yeah, our practice of putting Berger and Haupt ashore on those French beaches wasn't easy. Berger kept demanding that we go in closer to shore before his raft was launched. Good thing we didn't or our new U-boat would still be grounded on some sand bar."

"Berger complained about not having enough room on the boat, Hans. Wait until the provisioning gets onboard, along with the torpedoes and a full crew...he'll know what close quarters on a U-boat is all about."

"Haupt is more relaxed than Berger." Hans looks around to make sure there isn't anyone within earshot and adds, "Haupt doesn't come on like a staunch Nazi, like Berger does."

"Wonder if Berger is getting upset because I fail to return his 'heil Hitler' salutes. Anyway, the boat operated well during sea trials, Hans." Heineke looks up at the new antenna mounted on the conning tower and says, "That prototype *Naxos* short-wave radar detection device tested well. We were able to get a warning signal from the simulated enemy aircraft radar before a sighting from our deck watch. This will give us time to dive if attacked by an aircraft."

"No more surprises from the air, Karl. But I've got some concerns about the device. When it's turned on, couldn't the signal tell an enemy destroyer or plane where we're located?"

"It shouldn't. It's a receiver and only listens...does not transmit."

Later, when Heineke is asking the supply oberleutenant in charge of provisioning for more water, based on the addition of the two saboteurs, a messenger approaches him.

Hans is now below, supervising the storage of provisions. Heineke shouts down to him, "Hans, the admiral wants to see me. You're in charge."

* * *

When Heineke arrives at headquarters shortly after, Adjutant Godt ushers him into Admiral Dönitz's office. The admiral stands and walks to the front of his desk. Before Heineke can go through the formal protocol of saluting and reporting as ordered, Dönitz reaches for his hand and then gestures toward the brown leather couch.

"I've summoned you here for several reasons," Dönitz says.

"First, although I've had some preliminary reports, I want to know how the sea trials went with that new *Naxos* device."

Heineke briefs him on the test results.

"Very well. I'm losing too many U-boats by aircraft attack. You'll have the prototype on board U-*582* and I'll need some success there before I go to Hitler for the funding of *Naxos* and some other technological advances for my U-boats. The Americans have improved their submarine detection methods on the sea and in the air, and we need to find ways to counter them." A sad expression comes to the admiral's face when he says, "I've lost seven U-boats so far this month, and too many men."

As he says that, Heineke notices that the admiral looks more tired and tense than he did at their last meeting. Dark circles are under each eye and it appears that he's lost some weight from his slim frame. "I'll report the effectiveness of *Naxos* to you by Enigma, sir."

"Good. Now I must tell you, I'm calling off Operation Drumbeat on May 24. It was a success for six months, but now the American ships are leaving their ports in convoys, escorted by destroyer instead of sailing alone."

"We did have a good run for six months, sir."

"Yes, it was *a happy time*, Heineke, but the Americans have caught up to our tactics now." The admiral's glance goes to the large window and out toward Lorient Harbor before he speaks again. "Another item I'd like to discuss is your mission to launch the saboteurs." The tense expression on Dönitz's face eases into a smile. "I understand that Berger was putting a lot of demands on you to get in close to shore during the practice launching."

"Yes, sir, but I held him off due to the safety of the boat."

"Good, but I've got a lot of pressure from the very top to make his mission a success. I'm counting on you and your crew to do your part, Karl."

"Yes, sir."

"Alright, now, I must tell you that this will be your last patrol. As you know, I'll be moving my headquarters from Lorient to Paris soon. I'm going to put Kapitanleutnant Godt in charge of U-boat operations here at Lorient and I want you to assist him. He will be promoted to Korvettenkapitan. The Allies are making Lorient a prime bombing target. The city is taking a beating, but our thick concrete pens have yet to be penetrated. Godt will move his operations section from this building into a submarine pen very soon."

It takes a few seconds for Heineke to absorb the new duty assignment and the revelation that this is going to be his last patrol. "May I make a recommendation for my replacement to command U-582, sir?"

"Yes, but I've already thought about that. Wouldn't Hans Topp be the right one?" The admiral's eyes narrow as he seeks Heineke's with the next question. "Is he of stable mind after experiencing such a tragedy, losing his family in that Augsburg raid?"

"That would be my choice, sir. Hans is still deeply saddened by the death of his family, but has coped with the loss and is firmly resolved to do his duty."

"Good. He will be promoted to kapitanleutnant and he'll have command of U-582 when you return. Have a good patrol… put up with Berger. As I said, I'll be moving to Paris, but I may still be here when you return." Admiral Dönitz again looks out the picture widow at the submarine pens and Lorient Harbor beyond. "Your duty here will not be a pleasant one." He then turns from the window and adds, "If conditions get too bad later on in Lorient from the bombing and an enemy siege, Heineke, I trust you'll know what to do to take care of yourself."

Karl Heineke hears his first pessimistic words from the admiral, but he knows what they may imply. A vision of Marie Paul's parents' farm in Normandy suddenly comes to him.

* * *

When Heineke returns to U-582, Hans has just finished supervising the loading of eight torpedoes, six less than the normal allocation to make room for Berger and Haupt with their equipment.

"Hans, let's go to the bistro. I've got some good news for you."

"Is it that Berger's been replaced?"

"No such luck, but, anyway, I think you'll like what I do have."

When they enter Bistro Luis, the usual cheer goes up for their popular captain and his executive officer from the crew of U-582.

Just as they sit in a booth and order their beer, an air raid siren starts to scream its message throughout Lorient. The bistro owner has made some adjustments to cope with the frequent bombing raids of late and he's quick to herd his patrons down a set of stairs to a basement air-raid shelter—a fortified extension of the upstairs bistro with a bar, tables, and booths. The tunnel-like structure had been carved and blasted out of solid rock. At one time, the tunnel had been used as a wine cellar for a local grower to store large barrels.

Heineke and Hans are seated and served. They can hear the muted sound of bombs exploding above them as they rain down on the city of Lorient. Some would strike the impregnable U-boat pens, causing little damage.

Hans says, "Soon, they'll develop bigger, more powerful bombs that will penetrate the pens."

Karl uses Hans's comment as a lead-in to reveal the news. "Yeah, I'll be stationed here when those super bombs start hitting the pens."

Hans shows his surprise at that remark by halting his pint glass halfway toward a large gulp of beer and setting it down on the table. "This has got to be the news. Are you going to be assigned shore duty after this patrol?"

"Yes, in operations here at Lorient, and you're taking my place then as captain of U-582, Kapitanleutnant Topp."

A handshake by Heineke is followed by a hug. Soon, the word of Hans's pending promotion spreads among the crew and it becomes a good excuse for a party.

CHAPTER 31

May 15, 1942, Outside Boston Harbor

"Sir, I suggest we make port here to get that sonar fixed before heading to Charleston."

The *SS Roper* is returning after escorting twelve supply ships from several Southern United States ports to Halifax, Nova Scotia, where they will join with thirty-two others for a North Atlantic crossing to England.

Bill Childs's executive officer is aware of the relationship Bill has with Barbara Sheffield and that she's there in Boston, training to be a nurse. His suggestion comes to Bill with a wink of an eye.

Bill smiles and says, "Okay, Number One, we'll dock in Boston. How long will it take to fix the sonar?"

"According to the First Naval technicians, it should be repaired by fourteen hundred hours tomorrow and we can be on our way to Charleston by sixteen hundred."

After the docking procedure, Bill leaves his executive officer in charge and hurries down the gang plank in search of a pay phone. *It's Friday evening…would Barbara still be in Boston or has she gone home to East Bay for the weekend?*

Four ring tones bring an answer from a nursing student who picks up the phone in the dormitory corridor outside of Barbara's room.

After Bill asks for Barbara, the young girl says, "Sure, she's in her room. I didn't know at first who you meant. We call her *Mother Superior* here. She's a real brain and groovy…she helps all of us."

It takes a few minutes before she comes to the phone. "Bill, is that you? Where are you?"

"I'm in Boston, Mother Superior. How about a date this evening, or do you have a curfew at that convent?"

"I've got the night free. How long will you be here…where can we meet?"

"I'll be leaving tomorrow afternoon. One of my crew from Boston suggested Jacob Worth's restaurant. It's near your dorm on Stuart Street."

"Good, I know the place and love the food at Jake's, as my fellow nursing students call it. I'll be there in an hour. I've missed you so much. I'm starved and ready for some real food instead of those cafeteria offerings."

"Okay, can't wait to see you. I'll make arrangements for after dinner."

* * *

Bill is nursing a draft beer at Jacob Worth's long mahogany bar while waiting for Barbara. He takes in the atmosphere of the old establishment, noticing that the floor is covered in sawdust and the dining room tables are bare without tablecloths. The waiters wear tuxedos despite the austere décor surrounding them. He'd been told by that *Roper* crewmember from Boston that since it opened in 1878, Jacob Worth's has been a mainstay in the city. He looks up to see a portrait of the original owner, Jacob Worth, who came to America from Germany. Also hanging above the bar is a motto that proclaims: *SUUM CUIQUE*. Bill asks the bartender to translate the Latin for him.

"They tell me it means, 'Each his own,' sir."

Bill then scans the restaurant crowd. Despite any anti-German sentiments, he sees that it's filled with a mix of military and civilian diners enjoying the German fare.

As Childs is glancing at a menu, he feels a strong hug surround his back from the rear. He turns to find Barbara's smile. Then it's a long kiss, that's not thought very unusual by the Jacob Worth patrons. In this time of war affectionate greetings and goodbyes are common occurrences in public places.

They're led to a table. After being seated, they reach for each other's hands and hold them for minutes. Without saying a word, they gaze across the table and relish their closeness after being too long apart. Bill thinks she looks radiant with her brown hair pulled back. Also, those high cheekbones on that attractive face accentuate her large hazel eyes.

"Nurse's training must agree with you. You look great."

"Thanks, I really love it. I'm working with a surgical team now and it's where I want to be in a year when I graduate. But, Bill, tell me about your sea duty. You look so tanned and fit."

"I love the action and the command responsibility." He glances around the restaurant and lowers his voice. "Three U-boats have been sunk by the *Roper* off the East Coast since I've been commanding it. But tell me, how're things on your home front...Allie and all...Danny in the Pacific?"

"Allie's fine. He's a freshman and doing well in school. I talk to him a lot on the phone and see him on most weekends. Oh, and his beach patrol duties will end in a couple of weeks...on May 30. He knows about us and is okay with it. Danny and Jane also understand my situation. Jane has graduated from Boston College and accepted a job in Washington, D.C. at the Pentagon. Danny is in love with flying and with a few Navy nurses. I worry about him, though.

He's shot down four Japanese planes and I hope he doesn't take too many chances trying to get the fifth so he'll become an ace."

"What's new with the doctor and Lois Cohen?"

"I wrote to you about the sad news that Ernest Cohen was killed in action. There wasn't a long mourning period for Lois. Well, from what I hear, there's no change in their affair. In fact, it's very public now. I plan on a legal separation followed by divorce."

"When will that happen?"

"Well, that's the key question, isn't it? The separation has already happened and the divorce will follow. I've done some thinking on that and I just don't want to get bogged down with the divorce procedure until after I graduate."

Bill's response is interrupted by the waiter. They select a white pre-war Mosel wine from Germany that had been stored in the Jacob Worth cellar since 1938. They both decide to order wiener schnitzel, a special German veal dish, for the main course.

The waiter leaves the table with the order and returns with the bottle of Mosel. After Bill performs the wine acceptance ritual, he pours it into their two glasses. The meal is served. Barbara takes her first bite of the tender veal covered with the house special batter and then follows it with a forkful of the German-style potatoes. "Delicious, real food after that bland diet that the cafeteria offers," she says. "I have a recipe for wiener schnitzel like this one. I'd like to cook it for you someday and have you select a great California wine to go with it."

Bill smiles, pleased by her pleasure in the food and her offer to cook for him someday. He raises his wine glass in a toast, touching hers, and says, "So, will you marry me in a year and move to Santa Barbara, California?"

Barbara places her glass down on the table and reaches for his hand. "Wow, what a subtle proposal—but so waited for and wanted.

I love you and I accept your marriage offer, but that move to California is out until Allie graduates from high school. Anyway, Bill, you'll be away at sea until the war is over with."

"Not only are you beautiful, but you're sensible," he says. "I agree with your waiting on the move to California, but I still want to marry you after you graduate from nurse's training."

Barbara gets up from her side of the table and moves to Bill's chair. She holds his face in both her hands and kisses his lips. Tears of joy stream down her cheeks.

"Don't have a ring yet. All you have is the word of a sailor."

"I'll accept that word, and a diamond wouldn't go too well in East Bay on the finger of a still married woman."

Later, when they take the elevator from the Hotel Lenox lobby to the second floor and enter their room, she says, "This is wonderful. Look at this bed. It even has a canopy!"

"Yes, I may have gotten the last room available in war-time Boston tonight."

They hurry to undress and join together in that four-poster bed with the canopy on top.

Footnote: Barbara's recipe for wiener schnitzel may be found in the appendix B.

CHAPTER 32

The Dune, May 15, 1942

"No blue fish yet, guys. Maybe in another month we'll have those snappers and some stripers." As Junie says this, he makes his first cast with the change from a surf-casting lure to a bottom-fishing one.

After Junie sets his pole in its holder, he helps the others bait their hooks with wriggling sea worms.

Iggy recalls how Junie tricked him in the dune when he faked a comment from the medical journal about the symptoms of frequent masturbation making black hairs grow on a guy's palms. Iggy takes his chance to get even while Junie is skillfully baiting those hooks. He says, "Junie, you really are a *master baiter.*"

Junie chases Iggy into the surf while Allie screeches with laughter. After a few playful ducks under water by each boy, all three decide to go for a swim.

Later, at the water's edge their lines and lures are cast beyond the breaking surf. When the sinker-laden fishing rigs reach the bottom, they walk their poles back and place the butts into holders stuck in the sand. They then sit back on those three bleached-out, rickety beach chairs removed from the dune. They're silent while looking out at the ocean, enjoying the first eighty-degree day of spring, while occasionally eyeing their lines for the telltale tug by a flounder. The ocean is calm for as far out as they can see. It's hard for them to imagine an ocean war that rages beyond that horizon.

Iggy's pole is the first to bend and he hauls in a large one. He takes it off the hook and hands it to Junie, whom they call '*the fish surgeon,*' among the other names, noting that masterful skill announced earlier by Iggy. With his knife, he deftly cleans and filets the one-pound flounder and tosses it in a pail of ice, returning to his own pole in time to pull in the one on his hook.

After two hours of bottom fishing by the three boys, their catch totals fourteen flounder, filleted by Junie into twenty-eight pieces that are iced down in the pail, waiting to be fried. Allie lights the charcoal and places a large frying pan on the brazier grill.

A Coast Guard sailor on beach patrol stops by. He chats with the boys and reviews their catch. Iggy recalls that Scott Lee, the Coast Guard commander, requested an invitation if they ever did a fish fry. The Coast Guardsman calls his commander on the radio with the invitation from the boys to join them and he accepts, saying that he'll be at the dune in an hour with the 'hush puppies.'

Junie hears the radio response from Scott and says, "Well, when Scott gets here, we'll finally find out what a hush puppy is."

* * *

When Scott Lee's jeep pulls up next to the dune and he steps out, he's carrying a large, oil-stained bag filled with hush puppies.

"Hi, y'all. My Yankee cook at Highland didn't have a clue how to make hush puppies, so I gave him my mom's recipe."

Scott opens the bag and the three curious boys peer into it. They see small, round, golden-brown balls inside, which smell like donuts.

Iggy asks, "Why do they call them 'hush puppies,' Scott?"

"Well, I thought y'all would never ask." He grins and holds a hush puppy in his hand as he explains the lore behind the name. "Long ago, some good ol' Southern boys took to hunting with their hound dogs. They'd gather at a hunting camp or fishing camp and during the cooking of their meal, the hounds would start howling because those cooking smells drove their hunger. Well, the cook would be quick to fry up some balls of cornmeal batter, waiting to be used on the fish or venison, and toss it to the dogs. That would hush up those puppies. Now, hush puppies are part of every meal at all our fish fries in the South."

The bacon fat Junie adds to the large skillet starts to boil and he places four battered flounder filets in it. "We know why these little brown things are called hush puppies now, but since there are no dogs around, they look and smell good enough for humans to eat." He places several hush puppies to warm around the space remaining on the brazier.

Iggy stands by with paper plates as the flounder filets and hush puppies are ladled off the skillet for the first serving.

"Scott, these hush puppies are great. They go well with the flounder. My mom could make them. Do you have the recipe?" Iggy asks.

"Here, I made copies." He hands each of the three boys a mimeographed recipe for his mom's hush puppies. Scott then takes a bite of flounder and after he finishes chewing, says, "Well, now, y'all are short-timers. Two weeks from tomorrow, on Friday, May 30, you'll be doing your last beach patrol for this man's Coast Guard."

Scott looks to the Atlantic horizon and his thought is one of wonderment. *Here we are having a fish fry on an Atlantic beach on a warm spring day while German U-boats are torpedoing our ships not far out there in the same waters. It's a strange war!*

Footnote: Scott's mother's recipe for hush puppies may be found in the appendix B

CHAPTER 33

Outside Lorient Harbor
May 19, 1942

"Have our two passengers settled into our first-class accommodations, Hans?"

"Haupt has, but Berger's already used his ration of water and wants more. Haupt is relaxing on his bunk reading a book. The only questions asked by Haupt were if he could smoke his corncob pipe later on deck and if we could put him to work manning the new *Naxos* aircraft detection device. It appears that Berger has the start of some motion sickness."

The U-boat has cleared Lorient Harbor and is on the surface preparing to submerge for an extended time to avoid the destroyer and aircraft patrols from nearby England. They'll surface further out in the Atlantic to charge batteries and then set a direct course to Cape Cod, submerged except for some short intervals of surface charging.

"Berger will comply with our rationing rules, Hans. When we submerge, his motion sickness may subside. Tell Haupt to join me on deck for that smoke of his corncob before we dive. Also, I'll tell him then that we can use his engineering knowledge working with *Naxos* along with radioman Fritz."

Werner Haupt comes up on deck and stands behind the conning tower, out of the wind until his pipe is lit, before approaching Heineke near the starboard rail. "Good evening, Captain. Thanks for the chance to puff for awhile." This is said in English, as are most of the conversations between Haupt and Heineke.

"It's the least I can do, Werner, for one taking on such a dangerous mission as yours."

Haupt takes a long puff on his pipe. "We are both on dangerous missions." He looks out toward the horizon, where the sun is in its last throes of settling down behind some clouds it has painted red. "If I'm caught, I'll be executed by the Americans as a spy. And you, Heineke, are in danger of a depth charge finding the hull of your boat. Do you ever wonder why in the hell you've placed yourself at such high risk to die?"

"All the time, Werner. It's not that I'm a fanatic Nazi enthralled by my Führer, like a Berger-type is. I like commanding this submarine and taking the responsibility for it and my crew. I'm also fascinated by the advanced technology this U-boat offers me and I'm loyal only to my leader, Admiral Dönitz, who isn't driven by Nazi politics and cares about his men."

"Well, Heineke, I'm with you on most of that. I don't wave the Swastika around. I think our man in charge of espionage with his SS and Gestapo, Himmler, is an evil one. I observed a mass execution of some Jewish people while I was training in Poland."

"Yeah, things I came to know in Paris are making me believe that some of my countrymen are guilty of crimes beyond any humane level in history. But I'm curious, Werner…how were you convinced to be disloyal to the country you were born in?"

Haupt pauses, taking a long pull on his corncob before answering. "I'm an engineer and like the technical part of being a spy." He pauses to look up at the *Naxos* antenna array then to make sure he's not within earshot of the men on watch at the bow and stern. "I've never told anyone about the circumstances surrounding my so-called recruitment into espionage. At that time, one of Himmler's Gestapo interviewed me and subtly threatened that, as American citizens, my father and I would be sent to a camp for safekeeping unless I went to work for the fatherland in espionage."

"Are you still loyal to your mission, Haupt?"

He makes a mock "heil Hitler" gesture and answers, "Of course I will be loyal, Kapitanleutnant Heineke. I will carry out the tasks assigned to me for fear of that threat of reprisal action against my father by the Gestapo if I fail to do so."

"What's your feeling about Berger, Werner? By the way, this conversation shall not reach his ears."

"He's an ass, dedicated blindly to the Nazi cause. One of his duties as leader of the American espionage task force is to keep his eye on me for any signs of betrayal. In fact, Berger would've followed me up on deck if he weren't seasick. But besides his keeping a watchful eye on me, he needs me to carry out the mission of blocking the Cape Cod Canal while he's busy sabotaging ship-building at Fore River Shipyard nearby."

"Well, Werner, while you're on my boat, I'll keep him away from you as much as possible. And thanks for offering to monitor the *Naxos* receiver. It will help our radioman, Fritz Starnberg. We are now ready to submerge and take a heading for the East Coast of America, so come below with me and I'll introduce you to Fritz."

After the deck is cleared, U-582 submerges to a depth of forty meters and is cruising at eight knots. Heineke summons Haupt to the chart table to show him the plot on their heading of two hundred and sixty degrees toward the East Coast of the United States. He says, "Course corrections will be made later by sextant and then fine-tuned using the radio stations of Boston. Then we'll rely on the visual sighting of Highland Light at Cape Cod. Pass this on to Berger when he recovers."

CHAPTER 34

East Bay, May 22, 1942

Lt. Commander Scott Lee receiver this message from:

U.S. Naval Headquarters
May 19, 1942

U-boat strength in the North Atlantic has approached one hundred operational German submarines. Allied losses there continue at a high rate, especially among tankers. Admiral King has decided to order convoy grouping on the East Coast as well as blackout conditions in cities and towns near the shore.

* * *

"Well, it'll be Ignatius's last beach patrol next Friday night until Saturday morning, Gina. I'm glad it's coming to an end. The boys need to get involved with some non-war things like playing sports, going to dances, and so on."

"Next Saturday is Memorial Day, Betty—not a good day for Junie Cohen. The town is planning a ceremony honoring all the East Bay men killed and missing in action. That total is twelve now and it scares me because it's only been seven months since this war started."

"Yes, Gina, and our sons, your Marcello in England and my Larry in Hawaii, have yet to get into the fight. How many more years will this war go on?"

"Well, for some, the war is a blessing." Gina looks around at the overflowing crowd in the Oyster Shack, where she and Elizabeth Ann are enjoying a cocktail and nibbling on the free cheese and crackers, after their volunteer duty at the Red Cross. "This war has brought many new jobs to East Bay folks. Antonio's brother, Sal, the lobsterman, just got hired as a welder at the Fore River Shipyard in Quincy. They're running three shifts, seven days a week there, trying to build ships as fast as the German U-boats are sinking them. They've even hired some East Bay woman as riveters at Fore River."

"There goes my supply of lobsters, Gina. Sal was my source for them."

"Don't worry about that, Betty. His shift at Fore River is three to eleven and he pulls his traps in the morning before going to work."

"Speaking of lobsters, look at who's enjoying two of the same at that table by the window." Elizabeth Ann nods toward Doctor Sheffield and Lois Cohen.

"Oh, if it isn't the merry widow. My, that sounded bitchy, didn't it?"

"A little, but you'd think they'd be more discreet, Gina, especially with it only being a couple of weeks since she received that telegram."

"Have you heard how the other two lovebirds are doing?"

"Yes, I do have some news. It comes from the beach patrol boys. Allie told Ignatius and Junie that his mom is going to marry Bill Childs after she graduates from nursing school and then move to California after he graduates from East Bay High."

"She has to divorce the doctor before that happens."

"Yes, she does, Gina. I heard from that same beach patrol grapevine that she'll divorce him after she graduates...probably doesn't want to get involved with the divorce procedure until she finishes training. They're legally separated now and they've remodeled their house so that it's two separate apartments. I bumped into Barbara at the post office today. She's home for the weekend...looks happy and radiant. Being in love must agree with her."

"I wish her well. I've always liked that lady, Betty."

"Likewise, Gina." Elizabeth Ann takes a sip from the last of her Manhattan and stands up from the booth, looking at her wrist-watch. "Well, enough of this East Bay gossip for a while. I've got two hungry men to cook supper for. I'm frying haddock tonight and trying a recipe given to Ignatius by Scott Lee. It's something from the South called hush puppies."

CHAPTER 35

"We're approximately two thousand three hundred nautical miles out from Lorient, Hans, with about five hundred more to go to reach Cape Cod on the early morning of May 30." Heineke holds the sextant up to one eye, focusing it on a star. He takes a reading and says, "I'll double check our position on the chart, but I believe we're on course."

It's a clear, star-filled night and Heineke and Hans are on the deck of *U-582* with two other members of his crew who are on watch. They've been running submerged for a long time and the batteries are now being charged on the surface while they cruise at eighteen knots.

"We're getting within enemy aircraft range, Karl." Hans looks toward the two men on watch and says, "I've told them to be on high alert and Werner Haupt is manning the *Naxos* receiver below."

"What's Berger up to?"

"Ever since he recovered from seasickness, he's been a pain in the ass, demanding more than his ration of food and water, ordering the crew around, and hanging around the radio and Enigma, trying to monitor all incoming messages."

"I've told Fritz to bring all radio and coded Enigma messages to me before he gets them." Heineke takes one more sighting with the sextant and says, "I'm going below to take a look at the charts, Hans. I'd like you to stay here with the deck watch. We'll be running submerged in three hours from now and we'll stay that way until we're off Cape Cod."

When Heineke is below at the chart table making sure of his course, Berger approaches him and asks, "Where are we?"

"Right here, Berger." Heineke points to a place on the chart. "We're proceeding on course and we'll be off Cape Cod early Saturday morning."

"Good. I'll expect you to launch us no more than a hundred meters from shore."

"I'll bring you in as close as possible, Berger, within safe conditions for my boat and crew."

"Your boat and crew are not as important to the fatherland as my mission."

"Look, Berger, I've had enough of your..." Heineke is interrupted by Werner Haupt, who's monitoring *Naxos*.

Haupt is holding an earphone to his ear with one hand and fine-tuning the *Naxos* receiver dial with the other when he yells out, "I have a signal from an enemy aircraft's radar!"

Heineke immediately responds with, "Alarm!" A command to clear the deck is then sent to Hans Topp by the U-boat interphone. The two deck watchmen scramble down through the hatch, followed by Hans, who turns the wheel to secure it.

Heineke gives the command to the helmsman to crash dive and then orders the rest of his crew to move fast toward the bow. Berger hesitates, blocking the way, and is pushed forward by Hans.

"Level off at one hundred meters, Helm."

The helmsman responds to Heineke's command and when the depth gauge reads one hundred meters, he positions the hydroplanes to level U-582 there. The concussion from bombs detonating fifty meters above rocks the U-boat, but they're too far away to cause any damage. Three more passes by the aircraft come with the same results.

After there's no explosion sound for ten minutes from the water above the sub, Heineke says, "Their bombs are set to detonate at a U-boat's initial crash dive depth." He looks over at Werner Haupt. "The *Naxos* device gave us enough advance warning so we could dive deeper before the plane was upon us. Thanks, Werner, for working it."

Berger says, "You will no longer use agent Haupt to monitor *Naxos*, Heineke. He must prepare for our mission and be under my command only." Berger looks over at the radio section. "By the way, I expect all messages coming in from *Enigma* or radio to be brought directly to me." His right arm then goes up in a rigid salute as he says, "Heil Hitler." Berger waits for Heineke's return salute in kind and when he doesn't get it, he turns abruptly on his heels and walks away, motioning to Haupt to follow him.

Heineke directs the helmsman to take U-582 up to forty meters and maintain the heading toward Cape Cod. He leans over to whisper into the radioman's ear. "Fritz, I repeat…after you decode all messages, including those from the SS for Berger, I want you to bring them directly to me."

Gulf of Maine, 1p.m., Friday, May 29, 1942

U-582 surfaces for the last time before it will be off Cape Cod at 3 a.m. on May 30. Hans and Heineke are on deck with three of the crew on watch.

"This has to be only a short time on the surface, Hans. We're only about eighty miles off the coast of northern Maine." He makes a quick reading with the sextant aimed at the sun. "We're about a hundred and thirty miles from our launch position and we'll be there easily within twelve hours. I'll use the radio stations of Boston to make sure of our position. We should be able to pick up their broadcast from here."

They go below. Werner Haupt is sitting with Fritz at the radio.

"Fritz, scan the antenna for a strong radio signal from a Boston station and give me the coordinates where it peaks."

Werner puts on a set of earphones monitoring Fritz's activity and in a few minutes a smile comes to his face. He says to Heineke in English, "Man, listen to this jazz. It's making me homesick." He hands the earphones to Heineke. Karl listens for a minute while Fritz zeroes in on the Boston radio signal. The disc jockey changes the jazz record to a popular tune. Heineke hears a song with the lyrics, "You'd be so nice to come home to," and Marie Paul's face flashes through his mind, as well as the thought, *Will I ever make it home to her through this war?*

Fritz hands Heineke a note with the coordinates of the Boston stations written in degrees, after he gives the order to clear the deck and submerge. Heineke goes to the chart table to verify their position and course to Cape Cod.

* * *

Later, in the evening, while Heineke is in the captain's nook trying to get some sleep before the launch of Berger and Haupt early the next morning, Fritz comes to him with a message that he just decoded from *Enigma*. It was sent by the SS and addressed for Berger's eyes only. Heineke sits on the edge of his cot and starts to read it.

MAY 29, 1942

FOR: AGENT HERMANN BERGER'S EYES ONLY
FROM: SS MISSION COMMANDER RICHMAN
SUBJECT: AGENT HAUPT

THIS IS TO INFORM YOU OF THE SUDDEN DEATH OF WERNER HAUPT SENIOR IN MUNICH BY NATURAL CAUSES (A HEART ATTACK). UNDER NO CIRCUMSTANCES ARE YOU TO INFORM AGENT HAUPT OF HIS FATHER'S DEATH. YOU ARE TO INCREASE SURVEILENCE ON AGENT HAUPT IN CASE HE HEARS OF THE DEATH FROM ANOTHER SOURCE. AGENT HAUPT IS IMPORTANT TO YOUR MISSION AND THE REASONS THAT HE MUST NOT BE INFORMED SHOULD BE OBVIOUS TO YOU.

RICHMAN

Heineke finishes reading the message and says under his breath, "The bastards." He then speaks to Fritz, who stands waiting for his response. "Tell no one about this message, Fritz. I will inform Werner Haupt at the right time."

"Yes, sir. I'll not let that news get to anyone. I've become fond of Mr. Haupt and I'm saddened by his loss and the apparent hold the SS has over him."

CHAPTER 36

The Beach Patrol
Friday Evening, May 29, 1942

"Wow, when that sun went down, it got awful dark along this beach, Allie."

Allie presses the talk button on his radio to respond to Iggy's transmission. "Yeah, it's the same on my end. There's no moon tonight. If it wasn't for that flash every once in awhile from Highland Light, I'd be in total darkness here."

"Wish we could use our flashlights, but that blackout rule won't let us turn them on unless it's an emergency."

"As Junie told you before, Iggy, the boogieman is not going to get you."

"I wish Junie was here but, with all the Cohen relatives visiting for the Memorial Day ceremony tomorrow, he had to stay home."

"So, it's just us on this beach until six in the morning, Iggy. Do you want to swap every couple of hours...you take the Highland Light section and I'll do the P. Town stretch?"

"Nah, I'll stick with the P. Town one."

"Okay, see you in the morning unless we bump into each other in the dark. Watch out for the P. Town boogieman."

CHAPTER 37

"There it is, Hans…Highland Light. It's about five miles to the west of us. We'll launch the men right off the beach two miles north of the lighthouse at three o'clock then we'll get the hell out of there."

They surfaced and the crews on deck and below are getting ready to launch the two saboteurs. Two crewmembers are using a quiet compressor to inflate a large rubber raft. Those same men will paddle Berger and Haupt to shore and then return to the boat. They practiced the launching many times on the beach near Lorient and the real event had gone off very well.

"Karl, the raft and men are ready to launch."

"Good, Hans, I need you to keep Berger busy and away from me when he appears on deck. I need to speak to Werner Haupt alone."

"Okay, I'll bring him to the bow and point out his landing place."

Berger and Haupt appear on deck with their equipment packed in two sea bags. The canvas duffels are handed to the two paddlers, who place them in the rubber raft that's now tied alongside U-582.

Hans leads Berger to the bow and Heineke approaches Werner, who is standing above the raft amidships.

A little above a whisper, in English, Heineke says, "I have some sad news. Your father passed away."

"What!"

Werner says that too loud and Heineke puts his index finger up to his lips, asking for quiet. He then tells Werner about the message from the SS to Berger, instructing that he was not to be informed of his father's death.

"I did not show that message to Berger," Heineke says.

A tear appears on Haupt's cheek. With an abrupt swipe of his hand, he wipes it away and his sadness turns into anger. "Those SS bastards didn't want to lose their hold on me. Okay, we'll see about this mission of theirs."

"I'm sorry about your father, Werner. Now, you'll have to do what's right for you."

Werner Haupt shakes Heineke's hand and says, "Thank you, Karl." Still holding on to Heineke's hand, he adds, "If they find out that you withheld the message from Berger, the Gestapo will consider it a treasonable act on your part."

"I've dealt with the Gestapo before with Admiral Dönitz's help and I do not fear them," Heineke says. "Anyway, I consider you one of my crew, my *Naxos* operator, and worth that risk. Now, get into the raft that will soon land you on the shore of your country."

Werner releases Heineke's hand and climbs into the raft before saying, "You are a true friend...stay safe for the rest of this war."

"Sir, we are approaching the launch position and all is in order. We are taking depth soundings and have two meters of water under the boat."

"Thank you, Boatswain. Let me know when you have one meter."

In less than a minute, the boatswain's mate calls out, "One meter, sir."

Heineke then orders the helmsman to come about so that U-582 will be positioned broadside to the beach.

"Ready to launch," is Heineke's next command, followed by a protest from Berger.

"We are too far out. I order you to go in closer, Captain."

"Berger, get in that raft before I throw you in. I've only one meter of water under this boat."

"As you wish, but I'll report your insubordination to my SS superiors."

Heineke's next words are too soft for Berger to hear. "Only if you survive, Mr. Saboteur."

Before getting into the raft, Berger turns and presents his last "heil Hitler" salute.

The raft is untied and Berger and Haupt are on board with their sea bags filled with implements of sabotage. The two crew-members paddle the raft toward the shore of East Bay, Cape Cod, where a vehicle on Shore Road awaits the saboteurs.

CHAPTER 38

Iggy is about one hundred yards up the beach from Haupt and Berger when he hears their muffled voices as they get out of the rubber raft. He slowly walks toward the sound until the darkened outlines of two figures appear, wading toward shore in the moonless surf. His heart beats even faster when he gets a glimpse of the raft up on a wave as it returns to the U-boat. His mind races: *Should I run and hide?* Then he looks at the Auxiliary Coast Guard band on his right arm. *No, I'm supposed to question the people who are on this closed-off beach.*

Iggy approaches Haupt and Berger, who do not see him until they're surprised by his flashlight shining on their faces. "Who are you?" Iggy asks in a voice that quivers.

"Oh, hi…our fishing boat ran aground," Berger says, in heavily accented English. He moves closer to Iggy and notices his armband.

"What's the name of your boat?" Iggy stammers. "My dad's a fisherman and I know most all of them. Why did that raft drop you off and leave?"

Berger moves with swift purpose. He grabs the flashlight that shines in his face with one hand and Iggy's radio with the other, and tosses them twenty yards out into the surf. Then he reaches in his leather coat and pulls out a Ruger pistol and points it at Iggy's face.

Werner hears the safety click off. "Stop, Berger, he's only a kid!"

"This American Coast Guard Auxiliary kid can ruin our mission," Berger says. He then lowers the gun to his thigh. "Okay, what's your name, kid?"

201

Iggy is shaken, but manages to blurt it out. "My name is Ignatius Broderick, but everyone except my mother calls me Iggy."

The SS protocol is to offer a bribe if they were detected during their mission, so Berger reaches in an inside pocket of his long leather coat and his left hand comes out holding a wad of bills. He's in a hurry after seeing flickering lights out on Shore Road, indicating that their car is waiting, so he hastily grabs a bunch of bills and hands them to Iggy. "Here, take this five hundred dollars and forget you ever saw my face."

With the same hand, he grabs Iggy's shoulder and squeezes it hard. "Iggy, if you don't forget that you saw us, I'll find you and kill you."

"Let's go, Berger," Werner says. "The car is waiting."

They pick up their sea bags and leave at a trot through the dunes toward the waiting car parked off Shore Road.

Iggy pockets the money and waits until they're out of sight before taking off on a run down the beach toward Highland Light. As he starts running, he glances over his left shoulder past the breaking surf and notices the darkened silhouette of an object close to the waterline moving slowly out to sea. To Iggy it looks the same as that U-boat that took his dad's fish. After about a mile running hard, he meets Allie walking toward him along the beach.

"Jesus, Iggy, you look like you've seen a ghost," Allie says. "Where's your radio and flashlight?"

Iggy catches his breath and then manages a few words. "Maybe it was Germans from a submarine!"

"What! Where?"

Iggy points up the beach toward Provincetown and says, "Give me your radio, Allie." He reaches the Coast Guard duty officer at the Highland station and reports the bizarre happening.

Okay, Iggy, I'll wake up Lt. Commander Lee. Stay right there and wait for him."

CHAPTER 39

The rubber raft returns to U-582 and the crew is quick to deflate it and store it below. The deck is cleared and the U-boat gets underway on the surface, reaching a speed of eighteen knots. The bow is pointing to the east and it's a fast retreat from the shores of Cape Cod. After three miles on the surface at that get-away speed, Heineke gives the order to submerge.

"That flashlight beam we saw near their launch site, Hans, may have meant that our spies were detected. I thought the intelligence report, told to us by Berger, indicated that there wasn't a beach patrol."

"They could've gotten it wrong, Karl. What's your plan to escape these waters?"

"We'll submerge and stay underway in an easterly direction for four hours just in case that flashlight beam might mean there's an alarm to our presence and we're about to be chased."

"Okay, let's find some targets and have you complete your last patrol in a blaze of tonnage glory," Hans says. "We have eight torpedoes ready to launch."

Fritz interrupts them. "Sir, I sent the message to Lorient about the launch being successful and they came back with this order." He hands the message to Heineke.

Heineke reads it. "We're to head for the Caribbean, Hans, and we'll meet a milk cow for provisions." He gives the message that shows the rendezvous coordinate and the length of time they'd be on patrol in the Caribbean to Hans.

"Calmer and warmer waters for us, Karl, and with milk cow provisioning, it will make for a long patrol."

"Yes, we'll not be back in Lorient until July 5, according to this order. Hans, tell the cook that as soon as we're off shore about eighty miles, I want the crew to be given extra rations to reward them for the successful launching of the saboteurs…including extra water and a dinner of sausages, potatoes, beets, and carrots."

"Yes, sir, and perhaps a celebration is in order for getting rid of Berger. But, Karl, I hope we don't miss the milk cow rendezvous. I couldn't stand that fish chowder diet again."

CHAPTER 40

Fifteen minutes after Iggy's radio call, the Coast Guard jeep brakes next to the boys, kicking up a cloud of sand. Scott Lee's hair is uncombed and when he gets out of the jeep, he's buttoning his uniform.

"Iggy, tell me what happened."

In quick, breathless bursts, the words come from Iggy describing his encounter with the men.

"Okay, I've heard enough for now. Jump in the jeep and show me the place where you saw these guys," Scott says. Then he speaks to one of his men sitting in the jeep as he drives off down the beach.

"Murphy, get on the radio and tell the duty officer to contact the FBI and Naval OSI as well as Coast Guard command that we have a suspected landing of German spies here by U-boat. Also, tell him to get a hold of Peter Broderick, Iggy's dad. I want him here on the beach. Oh, and let it be known that the two men were picked up by a vehicle on Shore Road and proceeded in the direction of East Bay center about a half-hour ago. If they're headed off cape, suggest that the state police set up road blocks at the canal bridges."

Iggy directs the jeep to the place on the beach where the men landed. His radio and flashlight have washed up nearby plus are rolling in the surf until one of Scott's men retrieves them. Two other jeeps and a weapons-carrier vehicle arrive, filled with Coast Guardsmen. They spread out, looking for evidence along the tracks made by Haupt and Berger through the dunes on their way to Shore Road.

The headlights of Peter Broderick's pickup truck appear racing down the beach toward them. The truck comes to an abrupt stop, and Peter jumps out and rushes toward his son. He kneels in the sand next to Iggy and his arms surround him in a hug. "Are you okay, son?"

"Yeah, I was scared before, Dad, but I'm alright now."

Scott Lee is on the radio talking to his area Coast Guard commander. After, he leaves the jeep and comes over to Iggy and his dad. He shakes Peter's hand, saying, "I'm sorry about this, but your son did everything right. There's not much we can do here anymore and I just got an order to get back to Highland Light. Looks like it's going to be a full-blown dog and pony show for the brass, FBI, OSI, and state police. They'll be here in a couple of hours when they arrive from Boston. They want Iggy to brief them on the details of his encounter with the men and a description." He looks over at Allie, who's standing next to the jeep. "Allie, you're relieved. My men will finish your patrol and you can come with us to Highland." Scott grabs Iggy's shoulder in a soft squeeze and looks toward Peter Broderick. "Will that be okay with y'all?"

Iggy nods his head. Peter says, "Let's get done with it."

"Good, your breakfast is on me before that big ol' meeting. I'll have my cook fry up some eggs and Georgia ham with a mess of grits from my mom's recipe."

The adrenalin rush has made Iggy hungry for that breakfast Scott mentioned. On the way to Highland Light in the pickup truck, he asks, "What're grits, Dad?"

"It's some kinda Southern food, son."

Iggy smiles for the first time after his scary episode on the beach and says, "That figures."

Footnote: The recipe for grits may be found in Appendix B

CHAPTER 41

"That's not good," Otto Kittel says after Berger tells him about their confrontation with the kid belonging to the Auxiliary Coast Guard. "If your bribe and death threat does not silence him then an alert will be sent to the state police and they'll block the bridges over the canal so we can't get to Quincy."

They've just passed through Orleans. Berger and Haupt are in the backseat of the Packard, Otto Kittle, alias Arthur King, is driving, and Wilhelm Rudorffer, alias William Rodder, is in the front with Otto. Their first stop is to drop off Werner Haupt with Wilhelm Rudorffer in the town of Sandwich bordering the canal. Then Berger and Kittel planned to cross over a Cape Cod Canal bridge and proceed toward Quincy.

"It was great intelligence on your part, Otto, telling the SS that there wasn't a patrol along that beach." After his sarcastic remark, Berger scowls toward Otto's thick neck and asks, "What now, you idiot?"

Werner stops puffing on his corncob pipe while thinking about the direction he'll take now that the Gestapo's threats relating to his father are over. He says, "Hold it, Berger. Your fingerpointing isn't going to help the situation we're in. We need another plan."

Wilhelm Rudorffer has been the quiet one until he says, "We have a motorboat at our disposal that will be used when Werner and I dive to attach the explosives to the ship that'll block the canal. We can use it to cross Berger and Otto over from Sandwich to avoid the bridge roadblocks. After I make a call to one of our

207

people, he'll meet you on the other side and take Berger and Kittle to Quincy by car. This Packard will then be available for Werner and me in Sandwich during our mission."

"Do you have our new identity documents, Otto, or did you foul that up also?" Berger's voice carries his mocking intent.

Otto doesn't answer Berger's question; Wilhelm does. He hands Berger and Haupt each a manila envelope containing the forged documents. "Haupt, you're a Norwegian sailor by the name of Stanley Johansen whose ship was torpedoed. You're recovering and waiting for a billet to sail out of Boston. And, Berger, you're a ship-yard worker who left Sweden before the German occupation. Your new identity carries the name Jasper Jergman. You'll find passports, driver's licenses, references, maps, and American currency in the amount of one thousand dollars, in twenty-dollar bills, in those envelopes."

In the town of Chatham, they spot an outdoor phone booth and Wilhelm makes his call to contact the man who'll meet Berger and Kittel at a canal overview parking place across from Sandwich.

* * *

The sun is just coming up when they reach the place where the motorboat is moored on the canal. Wilhelm had tucked fishing poles and fishing gear under the seats for ostensible use when he and Haupt were on the canal. The four men launch the boat and Wilhelm starts the motor. Ten minutes later, they beach the boat on the other side of the canal.

Before Berger jumps out, he speaks in a sharp tone to Werner. "You must carry out your mission for the fatherland with efficien-cy. I'll be checking in on you…and, Haupt, remember your father's situation back home in Germany. Heil Hitler!"

Berger then runs up the granite blocks on the canal bank following Kittel to the parking place where the car that'll drive them to Quincy awaits.

Werner Haupt watches Berger leave and his thoughts trail behind him. *How did guys like Berger, with his Gestapo and SS cohorts, become such a bunch of inglorious criminals?*

CHAPTER 42

"That German SOB put a gun to your head, Iggy?"

"Yes, sir...until the other man told him to stop because I was only a kid."

Agent Sean Collins of the FBI, who's taking the lead in the investigation, asked Iggy that question.

Collins is a product of Boston College, where he played football. He's over six feet tall and broad-shouldered, with dark curly hair—a veteran agent, forty-five years old, in charge of the Boston FBI office.

They're seated around a table in the mess hall at the Highland Light Coast Guard station. The FBI agent is joined by Navy Captain Johnson, OSI Commander Grogan, and Captain Burke of the Massachusetts State Police. Scott Lee and the area Coast Guard commander, along with Peter and Allie Sheffield round out the group taking part in the meeting. Grogan and Johnson are the same men who were part of the boarding party that investigated the *Elizabeth Ann* piracy by U-boat.

"And he threatened you?" Agent Collins asks.

"He said if I didn't forget that I saw them, he would kill me. But before that he gave me a bunch of money to not remember them. He said it was five hundred dollars."

Peter lets out a deep sigh and swears under that same breath after hearing about the threat to his son.

The wad of bills has not been touched since Berger gave it to him. It is still tucked deep down in Iggy's pants pocket. He starts to reach for the money, but is interrupted by Grogan.

"Hold it, Iggy! Let's be careful with the money. The German's fingerprints could be on it. Let's get your prints first."

Grogan brings a fingerprinting kit out of his briefcase and takes Iggy's prints. Then he hands a pair of thin gloves to Iggy to put on before he withdraws the money from his pocket. Iggy reaches his gloved right hand into his pocket and it comes out with the wad of bills. He places the money on the table.

Grogan, with gloves on his own hands, starts counting the money. "Whoops, there's only four hundred and fifty dollars here…in nine fifty-dollar bills. You got short-changed, Iggy."

The tension breaks for a moment when those seated around the table laugh at Grogan's remark.

"Okay, I'll take this money to the lab for fingerprint and other analysis. It will be booked as evidence and after we get this guy and sentence him, it'll be returned to you, Iggy."

"Just like you returned my U-boat fountain pen," Iggy says.

"Right…and I hope we can stop meeting under these circumstances."

The state police captain, after talking to his dispatcher by phone, speaks to the group. "The roadblocks at the bridges didn't turn up anything. They're still on the cape or they crossed the canal by other means."

A barrage of questions then come at Iggy. Captain Johnson asks about the direction he saw the U-boat headed; Collins and Grogan want a detail description of the men and what they were carrying. The Coast Guard commander is curious about what he saw with his glimpse of the rubber raft. Then it is Collins who brings up Iggy's future security based on the threat.

Scott Lee volunteers to keep Iggy safe at the Highland Light Station for as long as necessary. "Is that okay with you, Iggy?"

"Yeah, but do I have to eat grits every morning for breakfast?"

That brings the second laugh of a tension-packed morning from those around the table.

Peter Broderick says, "I'm going fishing tomorrow morning and I'll be at sea for five days. School's out now...my son will be safe with me on the *Elizabeth Ann*."

Iggy's broad smile tells all of them his approval of that plan.

CHAPTER 43

East Bay, June 5, 1942

"Jesus, Mary, and Joseph, Gina...my son Ignatius, a fourteen-year-old, has had more contact with the enemy at this point than my Marine son, Larry, and your Army son, Marcello. Can you imagine that German bastard holding a gun to his head?"

"It's unbelievable, Betty. I hope they catch him and he hangs by his neck."

"The other German may've saved Ignatius's life by stopping the guy with the gun from pulling the trigger, but the threat by that German spy of killing Ignatius is still out there. As much as I didn't want him on the boat with his dad, he's probably safer there now than he would be here."

"Those Germans may be too busy doing what they came here for to go after Iggy, Betty, even if they do find out that he reported them."

Gina Posada and Elizabeth Ann Broderick are at the Red Cross Center doing their Friday afternoon bandage-rolling task.

"Gina, I need some East Bay news or gossip to take my mind off this."

"Well, I was at the services on Memorial Day and Junie Cohen stepped up to be handed a folded American flag by an Army captain. He looked so grown up in his suit and tie. Doctor Sheffield was standing with Lois, holding her hand throughout the ceremony. Danny Sheffield is home on leave taking part in a war bond drive across the country. He's what they call an, *ace*, after shooting down five Jap planes. He flew over the ceremony in formation with three other planes from Weymouth Air Station."

"Well, the affair between the doctor and Lois is pretty much out in the open now. Was Barbara Sheffield there, Gina?"

"Yes, and I got to talk to her. She looks happy and lovely, and was just bubbling with pride when they announced the thing about Danny being an *ace*. I was standing with her and Allie when Danny's plane flew over. Scott Lee was there and spoke to the crowd, commending the service Iggy, Junie, and Allie had performed for the Coast Guard doing beach patrols."

"I'm so glad they're finished with those patrols, Gina, especially in light of what's happened. We talked about this before, but I'd like to see them do normal high-school things now, like sports, going to dances, and enjoying their summers on the beach...fishing and swimming, free from the responsibility and the obvious danger of those night patrols."

"Well, they may just do that. I hear they can still use their dune hut without any beach restrictions, like the rest of us have, as a reward from the Coast Guard."

CHAPTER 44

Sandwich, Massachusetts
June 5, 1942

"Stanley, you have a phone call."

It still feels strange to Haupt to be addressed by his alias. Mary-jane Dodge, the owner of the bed and breakfast on Main Street in Sandwich, speaks softly after knocking on his bedroom door.

She told him earlier that her husband, a reserve naval officer, had bought the six-bedroom colonial house before the war with the intent of providing rooms for summer tourists. The only guest in the house now, because of the lack of war-time tourists, is Haupt. Maryjane's husband, Steve, will not return after the war.

Haupt opens the door and follows the attractive woman, who was widowed when the battleship *Arizona* was sunk by the Japanese at Pearl Harbor. She leads him down a flight of stairs to a phone in the foyer.

"Hello, this is Johansen."

"Jergman here," Berger says, while stumbling some over his own alias. "I've been hired by the Fore River Shipyard and I'll start work as an inspector tomorrow. Have you found a ship yet?"

"No, I'm still waiting for Rodder to assign one."

"Well, don't wait too long, Johansen." There's a pause before Berger asks, "I hope your father is doing well?"

Haupt wonders, *Has the bastard found out about his death?* Then he counters that thought with... *That's doubtful because there's no contact from here with the SS in Germany... as ordered.*

"He'll be fine. Thank you for asking."

"Yes, Johansen, he's in such very good hands. Oh, and call Rodder. He may have something for you soon. I'll be looking in on you. Bye."

Haupt places a call to Wilhelm Rudorffer, alias William Rodder, who lives in Sagamore with his wife and kids and works in a restaurant there.

Rudorffer answers after one ring. "I was just going to call you. Our man in Quincy is anxious for us to get to work. A ship from New York will be here tomorrow night, Johansen, and it's a good prospect for work. I'll meet you at seven tomorrow evening at your place."

"Okay, I'll see you then, Rodder."

Later, when Haupt is back in his room, thoughts run through his mind at a rapid rate. *It's time to turn myself in...they haven't got a hold on me. I can give the FBI that bastard Berger and more. I've got to get to the Boston FBI office today, and Wilhelm has the Packard. Perhaps Maryjane will take me there. I'll tell her I have a ship billet. We've become friends and perhaps more in the five days since I've been here...why not? I'll ask her for a ride to Boston and I may tell her the story of how I got into this.*

* * *

"It's kind of you to give me a ride, Maryjane."

"It's a good excuse for me to do some shopping in Boston, Stanley." Her long blond hair blows in the slip stream of the convertible, free of any restraint. Maryjane wears white shorts and a light blue halter that accentuates that same color in her eyes. She has the start of a summer tan on her face, arms, and legs. She glances over at Haupt to ask a question. "Do you want me to drop you off at some dock in Boston Harbor, Stanley?"

They've crossed over the Cape Cod Canal on the Sagamore Bridge and are heading north on Route 3 toward Boston. Haupt packed his few items of clothing in the same sea bag containing those would-be instruments of ship destruction. The sea bag is in the trunk of Maryjane's white 1940 Ford convertible. It is a warm day with all blue skies, and the top is down.

I hate that name—Stanley; I would've picked another alias if it'd been up to me. "No, Maryjane…not the docks. I have to make a stop at 100 Milk Street first."

"Oh, I know where that is. It's near Post Office Square. I can park and wait for you."

Now's the time to tell her…I'd like to see her again when and if I get through this. Our fast friendship could've developed into something more serious… the chemistry of attraction seems mutual, but we both didn't let it go any further. Perhaps it's her concern about it being too soon after her husband's death and mine because of my own circumstances.

"Maryjane, could you pull over at the next rest stop? I have some news about me that may take your attention off driving."

She looks over at him. "Are you going to tell me you're married?"

Haupt laughs. "No, it's nothing like that, but something that's even more shocking."

About a mile down the road, she pulls the convertible off the highway and into a rest stop. "Okay, time for that shocking news, Stanley."

He takes in a deep breath. "First of all, my name is not Stanley Johansen…it's Werner Haupt, and I'm not a sailor. I'm a German spy."

"And I'm Betty Grable. Is this some kind of joke of yours?"

"No, I'm serious." He outlines the circumstances: his threat of being sent to a concentration camp for safekeeping, the hold the Gestapo had over him because of his father, his father's death releasing that hold. Finally, he tells her of his intention to turn himself in to the FBI and implicate the other saboteurs before they can act.

"Wow, that's quite a story, Stan…I mean Werner. Am I your prisoner? Do you have a gun?"

"No, you're not a prisoner and I would never harm you, Maryjane. In fact, in the short time that I've known you, I've become very fond of you. And I do have a gun, but it's in my sea bag in the trunk."

Maryjane stares at the steering wheel for about a minute before she looks over at him and says, "Okay, I trust you…and no matter how strange your story seems, I believe it. Let's get you to the FBI in Boston."

CHAPTER 45

Maryjane pulls the Ford out of Milk Street traffic and over to the curb in front of the FBI Boston office at number 100. Werner jumps out and opens the trunk to remove his sea bag...then goes to the driver's side of the convertible.

"Thank you for the ride." He extends his hand and then decides that more of a goodbye gesture is appropriate. It's a quick kiss on her cheek. "When I get through this, I'll want to see you."

"Please come back to Sandwich...I'll be there. Good luck with all you have to do with the FBI." She then eases the Ford into traffic on Milk Street and drives away.

Haupt stands on the sidewalk with his sea bag slung over his shoulder, watching her car until it's out of sight and thinking about her invitation to return to Sandwich. He wonders, *Will that ever happen?*

Werner enters the building and tells a guard sitting at a desk in the lobby, "I'm here to see the man in charge of the FBI's Boston office."

"Well, he's here and his name is Agent Sean Collins." The guard looks at the sea bag slung over Werner's shoulder. "Are you a sailor?"

"Yes, and I have some evidence to show Agent Collins in this sea bag."

The guard points the way. "Okay, go up those stairs and his office is the first door on the right." He smiles and says, "A pretty lady by the name of Lucille is his gatekeeper. If you can get by her, he'll see you."

Haupt enters the office, where several desks are spread out around the room. Two are occupied by men in suits and the rest are empty. He walks to the far end of the room, where there's an attractive brunette seated at a larger desk with a typewriter, two telephones, and an *in* and *out* basket. The letters painted on a wooden plaque in front of the desk spell out *Lucille*.

Lucille looks up from a document she's reading and asks, "What can I do for you?"

"I'm here to see the FBI agent in charge."

"That's nice, but Agent Collins is a very busy man and you do not have an appointment."

"This is urgent business and I'm sure he'll want to see me."

"I'm not as sure." She looks at his sea bag and asks, "What's in the bag?"

"It's evidence."

"Very well…now what's your name and what's this urgent reason you need to see Agent Collins?"

"My name is Werner Haupt and I'm one of the saboteurs who landed on Cape Cod by U-boat last week. I'm here to turn myself in."

Lucille stands up from her desk and calls out to the two men seated at their desks. "Harry, Jim, I think you'd better come over here."

When they reach Lucille's desk, Jim asks, "What's up?"

"This man says he's one of those Germans who were put ashore by that U-boat in East Bay. He wants to see Agent Collins."

Jim takes the sea bag from Haupt and Harry pats him down for weapons, saying, "I'm going to put cuffs on him."

Haupt puts his hands behind his back and the cuffs click to the closed position.

"Okay, Lucille," Harry says. "Tell Sean we're holding him in the conference room for now."

She leaves and they lead Haupt into the conference room.

When Agent Collins joins them there, they have the contents of the sea bag spread out on the table.

"Wow! Quite a collection," Collins says. He looks over the items, including several electronic detonators, some paste-like substance in a gallon can, assorted diving gear, and a Ruger pistol. Collins grabs the pistol and checks to see if it's loaded. "Is this the pistol you held up to that kid's head when you landed in East Bay?"

"No, that was Berger. I told him to stop."

"We'll check that out with the kid. He got a good look at the both of you."

Collins takes a seat and says, "Harry, take the cuffs off. He's not going anywhere. Jim, Peter Broderick should be back in port at East Bay today. Get a hold of him and tell him we need him here with his son so that Iggy can take a look at this guy." He looks across the table at Haupt, who's rubbing his wrists. "Are you a United States citizen, Mr. Haupt?"

"Yes, I am. I was detained in Germany when the war started."

"Alright, Mr. Haupt, tell me your story."

Werner goes through the Gestapo threats that forced him to become a saboteur and recounts how his father's death released their hold over him. He tells them that Berger does not know about the death and has been continuing to threaten harm to his father since they were launched on Cape Cod.

"So, you turned yourself in as soon as your father died. How did you know that...and this Berger guy didn't?"

"I became a friend of the U-boat captain and when that message was sent to the U-boat by the SS while we were at sea, the captain didn't pass it on to Berger."

"Where's Berger now?"

"He's using the alias of Jasper Jergman. Berger is somewhere in Quincy with another guy, Otto Kittel, alias Arthur King. They start work at the Fore River Shipyard at three o'clock tomorrow. Their mission is to sabotage the ship-building effort there." Werner points to the gallon can on the table. "My task was to dive and plant this explosive below the waterline of a ship passing through the Cape Cod Canal to block it. That would make ships easy prey coming out of New York. The U-boats would then have their targets at the ready off Cape Cod in open ocean. I was to work with another diver…a man named Wilhelm Rudorffer, alias William Rodder. I know where he'll be at seven tomorrow evening in Sandwich."

"Good, we'll need you to identify those men when we round them up at Fore River Shipyard and in Sandwich." Then Collins locks eyes with Haupt for a few seconds and says, "I tend toward believing your story, Werner, but I can't make the call on your guilt or innocence. You'll have to tell your story to a federal judge and jury. The sentence for sabotage is death, but if you continue to cooperate I'll do my best to see that doesn't happen. You will be held for trial with the rest of them. Besides helping the FBI identify and round up the rest of the gang, there are other agencies that will want to pick your brains." He turns to Harry and Jim. "Get to Captain Johnson, Naval Intelligence, and Commander Grogan of OSI and tell them what we have here."

* * *

Three hours later, Peter and Iggy arrive at 100 Milk Street. They're led into the conference room by Lucille. It's now filled with Navy and Army brass, including Naval Captain Johnson and Commander Grogan of OSI. Those various agencies have spent two hours grilling Haupt about such things as sabotage tactics, U-boat technical advances, and SS/Gestapo operations. There will be much more to cover with him in the weeks to come, and they are counting on Werner's cooperation.

Sean Collins makes the brief introduction of Peter and Iggy Broderick to the group. "This is the brave Coast Guard Auxiliary lad who encountered the saboteurs while on beach patrol in East Bay." All the men at the table stand to applaud Iggy and his red blush of embarrassment makes it through all those brown freckles on his face.

Grogan and Johnson have met him on two other occasions and smile their greeting. Captain Johnson says, "We meet again, Iggy Broderick."

Collins gets to the point. "Iggy, do you recognize anyone around this table as being one of the men that you encountered coming ashore when you were on beach patrol the morning of Saturday, May 30?"

Iggy looks around the table and then points to Haupt. "That one looks like the man who told the other one not to shoot me."

"Good, Iggy. Now can you remember his exact words when he said that?"

"Sure, I'll never forget those words." Iggy points at Werner and says, "He said, 'Stop, Berger, he's only a kid.'

"Okay, Haupt, for voice recognition purposes as well as this boy's visual identification, I need you to repeat those words."

Haupt repeats the words and Iggy says, "Sounds the same as it did then, Mr. Collins."

* * *

The next day at 2:30 p.m., two FBI vehicles enter the Fore River Shipyard's front gate and park in back of the guard shack. Four agents exit one car, and Agent Sean Collins and Werner Haupt leave the backseat of the other.

The agents position themselves near the guard shack. Haupt and Collins are hidden inside the shack with a view of the time clock. Berger and Otto Kittle stand in line and then punch in at five minutes to three. Haupt identifies them and Collins signals his men to move in for the arrest. Their large lunchboxes are taken from the two men as they're patted down and handcuffed.

A look by Collins inside each lunchbox reveals metal filings and bottles of what he suspects could be a corrosive acid. Werner Haupt comes out of his hiding place in the guard shack just as Berger and Kittle are being led by the agents to an FBI vehicle.

Berger notices Haupt and scowls. "So, you're the informant, Werner." His next comment comes with a snarl of his lower lip. "Your father is a dead man."

"You're too late, Berger. Your threat is now dead."

After taking Berger and Kittle to the Nashua Street Jail in Boston, the two FBI vehicles head toward Cape Cod. Their plan is to capture Wilhelm Rudorffer when he arrives at Maryjane Dodge's bed and breakfast on Main Street in Sandwich for the purpose of meeting with Haupt at seven to conduct their mission.

The two unmarked FBI vehicles arrive in Sandwich at six-fifteen. The cars are parked on side streets away from the bed and breakfast. Four of the agents distance themselves, but have Main Street near the bed and breakfast within sight. They wait for the tan 1939 Packard that Haupt has described to arrive. Collins and Haupt ring the front doorbell.

Maryjane Dodge opens the door. She jumps a step back, shocked to see Werner. "Stan...I mean Werner, it's you."

"Yes, I told you I'd come back to Sandwich...Betty Grable."

The name she'd used at that rest stop on Route 3 brings a smile to both of them before Haupt introduces her to Collins, who explains what they're there for.

At six-fifty, the Packard pulls up in front of the house and Rudorffer gets out of the car. The four agents with guns drawn converge on Rudorffer and take him to the ground. After he's cuffed and led away, a fast look in the Packard trunk and backseat reveals diving gear, including two air tanks. One of the agents will drive the Packard to Boston where it'll be impounded as evidence, along with the contents of Werner's sea bag, the lunchboxes of Berger and Kittle, and the four hundred and fifty dollars given to Iggy by Berger as a bribe.

Haupt, Collins, and Maryjane watch the arrest through a front room window. Collins then leaves the house after thanking Maryjane for her cooperation. His intent is to give them some time together.

When he's alone with Maryjane, Werner says, "I'm going to be held in jail until the trial. I expect to be acquitted and freed afterward." He then looks into her eyes and asks, "Is it still okay if I come here after this is over?"

"Oh, yes, Werner…please do." She moves toward him and they hug. Then it's their first kiss before he leaves the house to join Agent Collins for the trip back to Boston.

CHAPTER 46

Hans Topp says, "Look at those bomb flashes on the horizon, Karl."

They're on the deck of U-*582*, sixteen miles from Lorient.

"Yeah, must be another raid on Lorient." Heineke points his binoculars in the direction of the flashes. "We best submerge in case those bombers have something left and are looking for a target on the way home."

Later, when the U-boat is fifty meters below the surface and they're in the captain's nook drinking coffee, waiting out the air raid on Lorient, Hans says, "Karl, you really did go out in a blaze of tonnage glory. During our last patrol in the Caribbean, we've sunk five ships worth thirty-four thousand two hundred tons with only eight torpedoes. That's worthy of an Iron Cross with swords and diamonds."

"I don't feel that glory, Hans. What I am feeling now is that we're destined to lose this war, along with too many U-boat crews going down. My next assignment in operations at Lorient is going to be a sad one, keeping score of U-boat losses while enemy air raids relentlessly bombard the submarine pens. And, Hans, I can get you an assignment in operations if..." His next words are interrupted by Hans.

"No, Karl, I still want to take U-*582* out on patrol. It's my home now since I have nothing else left."

* * *

Two hours later, U-582 slips into submarine pen number two at Lorient. There's no band waiting inside that fortified tunnel to welcome them. They're greeted by Korvettenkapitan Godt with a few men from his operations staff.

"Congratulations, Heineke, on another successful patrol. I'm authorized by Admiral Dönitz to present an Iron Cross with swords and diamonds to you." He places the highest medal for a U-boat commander around Heineke's neck and then steps back to salute him.

Heineke returns the salute and tells his crew standing on deck in formation to be at ease. He then makes a short speech, telling the crew of U-582 to perform well for Captain Topp. Then he asks if Hans would like to address the crew.

"I do have a few words," Hans says. "Let's all go to Bistro Luis for a cold beer."

A cheer echoes off the submarine pen walls as the crew approves of their new captain's suggestion.

The city of Lorient has been evacuated and few buildings besides those fortified submarine pens remain habitable. One of those few is the Bistro Luis, operating solely below ground now in that cave-like wine cellar.

Heineke and Topp find a table and Godt joins them with two men from his staff.

Heineke asks Godt, "Where's the admiral? I thought he'd be here until September before moving to Paris."

"There was another commando raid on the coast not far from here and Hitler ordered him to Paris earlier than planned," Godt answers.

After forty-seven days at sea in U-582, the crew and their present and former captains celebrate into the night to smother their fear of what the rest of the war will bring them.

CHAPTER 47

Three years later,
Lorient, May 1, 1945

Grand Admiral Dönitz sends his order of the day to the German Armed Forces after the suicide of Hitler in his Berlin bunker. Heineke and Godt are in operations at Lorient, reading the orders.

"'The Führer has nominated me as president of the Reich. I expect discipline and obedience. Chaos and ruin can be prevented only by the swift and unreserved execution of my orders…'"

After they finish reading the rest of his directive, Heineke asks Godt, "Günter, did anyone expect Admiral Dönitz to be nominated by Hitler as president of the Reich over the likes of Bormann, Goebbels, and Himmler?"

"Most likely the admiral didn't expect it either, Karl."

May 7, 1945

A flustered staff member bursts into the map room where Godt and Heineke are plotting the present position of what's left of the U-boat fleet in anticipation of their surrender to the Allies.

He blurts out, "Sirs, Admiral…I mean President Dönitz is on the phone."

Heineke and Godt go to the office, where there's a speakerphone connected to Dönitz's call.

Godt says, "Good afternoon, sir, and I might add congratulations…if they're in order."

"Hello, Günter. Is Karl Heineke with you?"

"Yes, he is."

"Good, I wanted you both to know that complete surrender of the German armed forces will take place tomorrow as commanded by me. As you know, I'm very close to my U-boat commanders and their crews. I'll expect you to issue orders that will prevent them from further harm. They are to cease all hostility and surrender. Arrangements have been made for our U-boats to be escorted by Allied vessels into Allied ports. Is that understood?"

They both acknowledge the order they've been expecting and finish plotting the whereabouts of each U-boat at sea.

"All right, gentlemen. After all boats have been located and directed to surrender, I want you both, as well as your staff, to take care of your well-being as best you can. And Heineke, Paris has not been ruined, like so many German cities…so start a life there with your mademoiselle as soon as you're able. Goodbye and God speed." Dönitz ends the call before they can respond.

"It's over, Günter."

"Yeah, Karl. As soon as we get the word to our boats, you're on your own."

"I think this last year has been the worst: Hans Topp lost with the crew of U-582; those British air raids dropping their five- and ten-ton *bunker busters* that penetrated our pens, making them non-operational; our last U-boats leaving here in September; the invasion at Normandy…it was then I knew we'd lost the war. I suspect that the *Enigma* code has been broken and the Allies have known the operational positions of our U-boats for some time. And here we are, hunkered down in a section of the only fortification standing at Lorient operations to surrender what's left of the U-boat fleet."

"Yes, Karl, but if it weren't for General Fahrmbacher and his garrison of fifteen thousand men surrounding Lorient to protect our operation, we would've been overrun by the Americans, who've now decided to bypass Lorient and rush to Paris…probably because Lorient is not worth a fight now. Anyway, Karl, the general will surrender tomorrow and we'll be on our own after that."

"We had our day, Günter, during Operation Drumbeat, but the Allied rapid improvement of their submarine warfare tactics was devastating to our fleet. I'm saddened by the loss of so many of our men."

"Yes, we both lost too many friends, and Dönitz has even lost two sons in this stupid war…his son Peter, when U-954 went down, and Klaus on a surface fast-boat attack on the English coast."

Günter Godt then turned toward a map of the Atlantic denoting the location of the remaining U-boats. "Okay, let's get our chickens safely into some Allied port and then you're free to leave."

* * *

It's 10 p.m. when Heineke finishes contacting the last U-boats, directing them to surrender. He orders U-873, U-1233, and U-234 to wait at a designated location for an escort into the port at Portsmouth, New Hampshire. It's his last act of a lost war.

The phone connections to Paris from Lorient have been repaired by the Americans so he calls Marie Paul to tell her that he'll make his way to her parents' farm in Normandy and will get to Paris as soon as possible. She suggests that he be escorted to the farm in Lesient, Normandy, by her brother in the Resistance to avoid any trouble from the Free French or American Army.

"It's better that you go to the farm for awhile anyway, Karl. Paris is chaotic with the American and French armies, along with all of the city celebrating. Where in Lorient can André meet you tomorrow?"

"There are only a few places left standing here, Marie Paul." Heineke thinks for a moment of where they could meet. "Tell André I'll be down in the cellar of Bistro Luis at noon."

"Okay. Oh, and bring Gretchen back with you when you come to Paris," Karl. I've just heard some very sad news about her parents that came out of that horrible camp at Auschwitz after it was liberated in January by the Russians."

CHAPTER 48

"This fish soup is delicious, Madame Bessette, and the white wine the best I've had in years, Monsieur Bessette."

Marie Bassette blushes, smiles, and says, "Thank you, Karl. I'm happy you like my bouillabaisses."

"It's one of the few bottles of wine from my vineyard that I was able to hide from the thirsty German and American armies," Paul Bassette says and then fills Heineke's glass with more of the wine. He raises his own glass in a toast and says, "To the end of all wars."

Heineke takes a sip and then lifts his glass and says, "To the end of a Nazi dictatorship."

Heineke is seated at a large oak harvest table in the kitchen at the farm of Marie Paul's parents, Marie and Paul Bessette, in Lesient, Normandy. Marie Paul's brother, André, who escorted him from Lorient to the farm, and nine-year-old Gretchen are also seated at the table.

Heineke will leave for Paris in the morning with André and Gretchen. He's been at the farm for two weeks, resting and gaining back some of the weight he's lost during the war by enjoying Marie Bessette's special dishes of Normandy.

Gretchen and he have taken long walks together through the countryside and he's bonded with the bright, inquisitive child. She's grown taller since they first met in Paris in 1942, and her jet-black hair is now shoulder-length. She heard rumors about the concentration camps from the other schoolchildren, and, on their walks, her expressive brown eyes have been sad when she peered up at Heineke to ask questions about her parents. Those concerned inquiries would have to go unanswered until Paris because the dire details of what happened to them are with Marie Paul.

After the meal, they leave for the parlor to listen to the news of the day. What Heineke hears on the radio disturbs him. Dönitz has been arrested and jailed after presiding as president of Germany for only twenty days.

He speaks of his shock to Monsieur Bessette and André. "I know Dönitz. He was never involved in Nazi politics or those rumored horrors implemented by Hitler. He concentrated on his military responsibilities and was a great leader of men."

"The victor's wrath has been so incensed by Nazi atrocities that they may reach out with very long arms to gather up even some of the innocent for trial," André says. After that, the tall, dark-bearded, and intense freedom fighter looks over at Heineke and adds, "I will take you to the French police and American authorities in Paris to make sure your part in the war is made clear and you are repatriated without prejudice."

* * *

The next morning, the 1937 black Citroen with André at the wheel, Heineke in the passenger seat, and Gretchen in the back enters Paris from the west, passing through Saint Cloud. Three blocks before they reach Marie Paul's apartment on Boulevard Saint-Germain, traffic is being held up and a crowd lines the sidewalk on both sides. They watch as a group of naked women with their hair shaved bald are walking in the middle of the boulevard. They are being taunted by the crowd.

Heineke suspects what their degrading march is about, but asks André anyway.

"These are the women, Karl, with whom the German soldiers that occupied Paris lived and fraternized."

As they pass by them in the Citroen, Heineke takes a deep breath and thinks, *I'm glad my visits to Marie Paul were careful ones or she might've been in that group.*

When they pull up to the curb in front of Marie Paul's building, Heineke Gretchen jump out of the car. He holds her hand as they race up the stairs. Gretchen is shrieking with joy. Marie Paul must've heard the clamor on the stairs. She's at the landing to greet them and surround both in her arms, with multiple kisses ensuing.

After the warm greeting subsides, André suggests they go to the authorities at City Hall to get Heineke repatriated.

"That's fine, André. Please make sure Karl is safe from any misconceptions." Marie Paul then takes Gretchen's hand and says, "I have something to tell Gretchen."

* * *

Karl and André return to the apartment two hours later.

"How did it go, Karl?" Marie Paul asks.

"With André's help, it went fine. His being a Resistance hero and vouching for me helped. Also, there didn't seem to be much bitterness toward the German Navy." He looks around the room and asks, "Where's Gretchen?"

"I had to tell her about the death of her parents at Auschwitz. She cried for awhile, but she's sleeping now."

"Okay, I've a couple of things to ask you, Marie Paul." Heineke takes her in his arms. "Will you marry me?"

"Of course I will." A tear rolls down one cheek before she asks, "What's the second thing you want to ask?"

"Would it be alright with you if we adopt Gretchen?"

She flings her arms around his neck and says, "I knew you'd want to do that."

"Okay, Marie Paul, wake Gretchen. We are going to celebrate the end of this war and our engagement with our daughter-to-be and André at Brasserie Albert."

CHAPTER 49

East Bay, August 14, 1945 (VJ Day)

"Can you believe the war is over, Gina? The Japanese have surrendered."

"Yes, and our boys made it back, Betty. Marcello's survived the Battle of the Bulge with shrapnel wounds in an arm and leg, and he fought the Germans all the way from North Africa to there. He's healed now and wants to buy a trawler with a GI loan and the money he's saved so he can go fishing with his dad. How's Larry doing? I bumped into him at Kline's Shoe Store and he looks kind of thin."

"He's okay physically, Gina, but after what he went through with the First Marine Division fighting the Japs on four of those Pacific islands, including Guadalcanal and Okinawa, I worry about his mental condition. Sometimes I catch him staring off in a trance. He doesn't want to go fishing with Peter and after those amphibious assaults in the Pacific, he may've had enough of the ocean. He just sits around all day listening to music on the radio. It's a program called the *Fifty-Two Twenty Club*, named after the twenty dollars the government gives each veteran for fifty-two weeks. But the good news is that he plans to enroll on the GI Bill at Boston College this January."

"Give him some time, Betty. After what he's gone through, he needs that to leach the horror out of his system."

Elizabeth Ann and Gina have finished packing clothing at the Red Cross Center to be sent over to Europe for the millions of war refugees. They're walking down Main Street, heading for the harbor. The people of the town that are milling around in the street look as if they're in the mood for a VJ Day celebration and are waiting for it to happen. Some men have started to build combustibles in a pyre, already reaching twenty-five feet high, at the corner of Church and Main.

"Since Peter and Antonio are out fishing and my Ignatius is on the beach with a gang of friends, including Junie Cohen and Allie Sheffield, you and I are going to celebrate VJ Day at the Oyster Shack, Gina."

The Oyster Shack is crowded for a Tuesday evening and when they're seated at the last table, Gina looks around and spots Doctor Sheffield and his wife, Lois. "That marriage seems to be going well, Betty...over two years now."

"Yeah, all the fuss and gossip around East Bay has died down. And it seems that both marriages worked out. I hear that Barbara is happy in California. She's on a surgical team at a hospital there. Bill Childs has retired from the Navy after twenty years and is working for the government. Allie Sheffield will go to California and start school in September at UCLA. He's staying here for the summer with his father. With the war ending, all three boys have abandoned their plans to join the military service."

"Hopefully there will not be another war to change that. Well, Betty, I guess it's 'all's well that ends well.' How about Jane and Danny Sheffield?"

"Jane is still in Washington, D.C., working at the Pentagon. Danny just got hired as a pilot for Eastern Airlines."

"Antonio saw your son Iggy drive by him on the clam flats with a dune buggy. Does it belong to him?"

"Yes, and you're not going to believe how he came by the money to buy it. Remember those German saboteurs that were launched out near Highland Light in '42?"

"Yes, one held a gun to Iggy's head."

"Right. Well, that same one tried to bribe Ignatius with four hundred and fifty dollars, and it was used as evidence during the trial. About two weeks ago, a check came to Ignatius from the FBI for four hundred and fifty dollars, and he bought the dune buggy with that."

"Wow, what happened to those two German spies, Betty?"

"Their trial was held, along with those of two accomplices. The guy that held the gun to Ignatius's head was Berger. He was their leader and was executed by electric chair. The two accomplices that weren't landed by the U-boat each got sentenced to twenty-five years in jail."

"How about the one that came ashore with that Berger guy, Betty? Wasn't he the one that saved Iggy from being shot?"

"Yes, his name is Werner Haupt, and he was freed after the trial."

"Was that because he saved Iggy?"

"That may have had something to do with it, Gina, but the real reason is that he was an American citizen and he helped the FBI capture the rest of the saboteurs."

"That's a fascinating story, Betty."

"And that's not all, Gina. After Werner Haupt was released, he married a girl from Sandwich named Maryjane Dodge. Together they run a bed and breakfast in Sandwich. He looked up Ignatius and came to his graduation from East Bay High in June...a nice man. He took us to dinner here at the Oyster Shack after the graduation."

"You did mention that Iggy and the Cohen boy, along with Allie Sheffield, are out on the beach. Are they celebrating VJ Day with other friends, Betty?"

"Oh, yes, among other things. It's a goodbye party for Allie, who's leaving for California in September. Also, Junie Cohen has been accepted to Harvard. He wants to be a doctor. Strange, all those boys were set on joining the service to follow their brothers, but the end of the war ended those plans."

"How about your son Iggy. Is he going off to college?"

"No, Ignatius wants to work with his father fishing on the *Elizabeth Ann*. With your Antonio leaving the *Elizabeth Ann* to buy his own boat with Marcello and my son Larry not wanting any part of going fishing, Ignatius will be first mate and take the boat over someday."

"Well, Betty, with the war years behind us, the folks of East Bay can return to the way they were before it came to disrupt our lives."

By the time they order the seafood platter and finish their Manhattan cocktails, the Oyster Shack is rollicking with a VJ Day celebration. It is as if a wave came through the building to wash away the pent-up tension that'd built up during four years of war.

CHAPTER 50

The Dune (VJ DAY)

"Where did Charlie Dwyer get the railroad ties?"

"He got them at the town dump, Junie."

"Good, Iggy, I'm glad they weren't ripped off from the railroad tracks."

They are building a bonfire with driftwood and other kindling, framed by those same railroad ties.

"Okay, time to tear down our dune and burn all except the canvas top. We'll use that to cover the seaweed when we steam the lobsters, clams, and corn," Allie says.

The old tent canvas is removed and the two-by-fours that held it down are tossed in with the other kindling. Those rickety old beach chairs are next to go in, along with magazines, comic books, and the orange crates that had held them. The bonfire won't be torched until after sunset, and in the meantime, there will be swimming, playing ball, and drinking Narragansett beer for the twenty boys and girls gathered on the beach.

The feast of lobster, clams, and corn will be held when the bonfire has dwindled down to embers. Then there will be layers of seaweed spread over the hot embers with those edibles on top for steaming, covered by the old dune canvas roof.

"Grab a beer and let's walk the beach like we used to on patrol," Junie says.

They leave the other kids and walk along in the direction of Provincetown. They're silent until they come to the place on the beach where Allie found the body from the *Cyclops* washed up.

"This is the place," Allie says.

They stop and stare at that spot in the surf for a minute and then move on to where Iggy confronted the saboteurs. They sit down in the sand there.

"I'll miss you guys," Allie says. "Maybe you can come to California for a visit. I knew you were going to be a doctor, Junie... probably a surgeon the way you filet those flounder and diagnose sprained and broken toes along with fingers at Kline's Shoe Store in the X-ray fitting machine."

After Allie says that, Junie gives him a light punch on the shoulder and they all get up from the sand and head back down the beach toward the stack of wood that will soon be a bonfire. When they get about halfway there, they see a Coast Guard jeep racing down the beach in their direction. Out jumps Scott Lee.

"Hey, if it isn't my ol' Auxiliary Patrol boys patrolling out of uniform with a bottle of beer in each of their hands. I came to say goodbye to y'all. I'm heading back to Georgia on the ten o'clock train. Probably stay in the Coast Guard Reserve, but this ol' boy has been offered a line coaching job at Georgia Tech." He gives each boy a fast hug and then his jeep is off down the beach in a swirl of sand.

When they reach the bonfire place, the sun has set and the other kids are anxious for it to be lit. Iggy lights the tall stack of wood and flames soon roar skyward.

"I saved this from the fire," Allie says. He hands Junie the medical dictionary he was always reading in the dune. There is a white bow tied around it. "Here, you'll probably need to read some other stuff besides all those good parts."

The three friends laugh as the flames from the bonfire flicker high up to reflect off Atlantic waters, where an ocean war had once raged too near.

APPENDIX A

Historical Facts

The non-fictional character Admiral Karl Dönitz is portrayed in this story with an overall fictional intent. But his German naval career and twenty-day term as president of the German Reich are real historical events. Dönitz spent ten years in prison after his trial at Nuremberg in 1946. Some have said that he was sentenced for doing his job too well. Dönitz died on Christmas day, 1980. A small group of survivors from his U-boat crews attended his funeral, but they were forbidden by the German government to wear their uniforms.

Some other incidents in this story track real-time historical occurrences. *The Eastern Sea Frontier Enemy Action Diaries* are notations of actual U-boat actions taken from U.S. Navy archives. Those real *Action Diaries* coincide with the timelines and events within the story. The raid on Augsburg by English bombers is another real incident that was placed in the story by the author at a time in phase with a fictional event.

The *Enigma* code device was used by the German command to communicate with the U-boats at sea. That code was deciphered by an English task force in England.

Three landings of saboteurs on the East Coast of the United States by German U-boats during WWII are well-documented occurrences. One took place at East Hampton, Long Island, New York, on June 12, 1942. Their mission was to destroy power plants at Niagara Falls and three aluminum factories. As they came ashore, launched by U-*202*, the two men were encountered by a young Coast Guard man on beach patrol. He was threatened and then bribed with five hundred dollars (when counted later, it was only four hundred and eighty dollars.) The Coast Guard man immediately raised the alarm and they were captured later.

The second incident involved a team of saboteurs that was landed by U-*584*, twenty-five miles southeast of Jacksonville, Florida. Their mission was to lay mines at several places, including the New York City water supply. They were all arrested by July 10, 1942, and ten were executed by electric chair.

The third launching of saboteurs was by U-*1230*. It took place on November 30, 1944, at Hancock Point, Maine. The two men's mission was to gather intelligence on the Manhattan Atomic Bomb project. The FBI was notified after Mary Forni spotted the two men walking in their long leather coats as she drove her Chevrolet home along West Side Road, returning from playing cards with friends. One man turned himself in and then implicated the other. They were both imprisoned for ten years.

The German naval Operation Drumbeat was a real WWII event, a successful operation contrived and orchestrated by Admiral Dönitz that sent U-boats to the East Coast of the United States to torpedo ships leaving ports laden with war supplies. The German U-boat successes came in the first year of their war on the United States East Coast, with devastating impact upon Allied shipping. Later in the war, U.S. anti-submarine tactics improved and German

U-boat losses were very high. The breaking of the *Enigma* code by a British task force enabled the Allies to gain valuable tactical information on U-boat operations. Unfortunately, for the German military their high command stubbornly refused to believe the *Enigma* codes had been broken.

At the end of the war, of the eight hundred and sixty-three U-boat total that went to war, seven hundred and fifty-six were lost, and of the approximately thirty-six thousand U-boat crewmembers, an estimated twenty-eight thousand were killed.

That aggression by the German U-boats during Operation Drumbeat was a significant enemy action that lasted only six months during WWII, but it brought the war very near to the United States homeland.

APPENDIX B

RECIPES
GINA POSADA'S RECIPE
FOR BAKE STUFFED QUAHOGS

* * *

Ingredients:

6 medium size quahogs (will make 12 shells when served)
3 tablespoons butter
1 large sweet onion (minced)
2 cloves garlic
4 medium-size potatoes
1/2 cup fresh parsley (minced)
3 cups bread crumbs
1/2 teaspoon cayenne pepper
1 teaspoon paprika
1 teaspoon celery seed
2 cups of clam juice (or as required)

Preparation:

Scrub quahog shells well and steam in a covered pan with one inch of water until for 20 minutes until they all open. Discard any that do not open. Remove quahog meat from shells. (save the 12 shells)

Boil potatoes, peel, and mash them. Remove stems from parsley. Peel garlic cloves and mince them. In a mixing bowl, combine garlic, seasonings, and parsley with breadcrumbs, and mix all until crumbs are fine.

Chop quahog meat until coarsely chopped. Add to mix of breadcrumbs and seasonings in mixing bowl. Melt butter. Mix it in with breadcrumbs and seasonings. Add mashed potatoes. Slowly stir in clam juice until mixture is moist but NOT soupy (the entire amount of clam juice may not be needed). Lightly oil quahog shells with olive oil.

Fill each shell with the mixture and sprinkle the top with paprika.

Bake at 450 degrees for 30 minutes, or until centers are cooked.

BARBARA'S RECIPE
FOR WIENER SCHNITZEL

* * *

Ingredients:

1 pound veal
1 cup of flour
2 eggs
½-tablespoon vegetable oil
salt and pepper to taste
2 cups of breadcrumbs
¼-cup of oil for frying

Preparation:

Cut veal into steaks about ½-inch thick. Mix flour in with
eggs, tablespoon of vegetable oil, salt, and pepper. Coat the
veal with that mixture then with breadcrumbs.
Heat ¼-cup of oil in a heavy skillet. Fry veal until golden
brown, about 5 minutes on each side.

HUSH PUPPY RECIPE
(from Scott Lee's mom)

* * *

Ingredients:

Vegetable oil for deep frying
2 cups flour
2 cups of cornmeal mix
2 tablespoons of finely chopped onion
1 cup of milk
1 egg, beaten

Preparation:

In a deep frying pan or deep skillet, heat 2 to 3 inches of oil until it boils. In a mixing bowl, combine cornmeal, flour, and onion. Add milk and egg; mix well and let stand for 5 minutes. Drop batter by tablespoon into hot oil. Fry until golden brown, turning several times. Take out and drain on paper bag. Makes about 15 hush puppies.

RECIPE FOR MRS. LEE'S CREAMY GRITS

* * *

Ingredients:

1 ½-cup of heavy cream
2 cups of chicken broth
1 ½ cups of water
5 tablespoons of butter
¼- teaspoon of salt
¼- teaspoon of pepper
2 cups of stone ground cornmeal

Preparation:

Bring heavy cream, chicken broth, and water to a boil in a medium sauce pan. Add butter, salt, and pepper. Slowly whisk in cornmeal and reduce heat. Cook 15 to 20 minutes over low heat, stirring frequently.Serves about 8